ECOS DEL MIEDO

Echoes of Fear

Horror Stories from the Heart of Latin America

Arturo Cova

First published 2026.

For those who grew up on horror movies and campfire stories —

and never quite lost the taste for being scared.

Author's Note / Nota del Autor

It started in seventh grade homeroom. Someone had left a copy of Goosebumps on the desk and I picked it up because there was nothing else to do and I did not put it down. That led to Stories to Tell in the Dark, and then to a very specific kind of obsession — the kind where you start looking for the next scary thing before you've finished the one you're holding.

What I discovered, growing up in Latin America, is that horror doesn't need a passport. A story about a weeping woman walking a river in Mexico lands the same way in Chile, in Colombia, in a seventh grade classroom anywhere in the world. Fear speaks a language that doesn't require translation.

That is what horror does. It becomes a language of its own. And like all languages, it carries inside it the history of the people who made it — what they feared, what they survived, what they needed to say when ordinary words weren't enough.

This collection is a small contribution to that conversation. Ten stories, ten legends, ten countries. I started working on them in 2012 and finished in 2026.

I hope many more come. From writers who grew up with these legends, who know them better than I do, who have things to say about them that I haven't thought to say. This is a beginning, not an ending.

— Arturo Cova, 2026

Contents / Índice

THE STORIES / LOS CUENTOS

01

La Llorona

The River Remembers

Ciudad Juárez / Rio Grande · September to January · 2026

The River Remembers

Marisol left at midnight.

Camila and Rubén asleep against her shoulders in the back of the coyote's truck, the colonia passing outside the windows, the lights of the houses she had known her whole life receding in the rear window. She had not looked at the rear window. She faced forward and held her children and did not look back.

Yesenia had not said goodbye. She had gone to her room and closed the door and Marisol had stood outside it for a long moment with her hand raised and had not knocked. The truck was waiting.

The coyote's name was Beto. He was nineteen years old.

— — —

The First Night — The Desert

They crossed the desert in two nights.

The first night was cold and black and vast. Marisol carried Camila on her back after the second hour. Rubén walked beside her without complaint, his knees pulled high over the scrub, a boy who had decided to be equal to whatever this was.

At 3 a.m. the wailing came from the east.

A woman's voice — not a scream, not a cry, but something that had moved past both into a third thing, a sound the body makes when it has been grieving so long that grief has become its resting state. Ay, mis hijos. The words carried across the dark scrub with no wind to carry them.

Everyone stopped.

The group stood in the cold and the dark and listened to the sound move — not toward them, not away, but alongside them, tracking the path through the desert as if it knew the route.

"Coyote," Beto said. "Sound carries weird out here."

No one moved for a long moment.

Then Beto walked and they followed, because the alternative was to stay, and staying was not the plan.

The voice did not stop. It stayed at its distance — forty meters east, perhaps fifty — and walked with them for another twenty minutes before it wasn't there anymore. Not fading. Simply gone, the way a sound is gone when the thing producing it has decided it has said enough.

Marisol held Camila tighter. Camila had not woken. Rubén reached up and found Marisol's free hand in the dark and held it and she held his back and they walked.

— — —

The Second Night — The Rain

The rains came on the second night.

Beto had not forecast rain. The sky in the desert does what it wants. The group crouched under an overhanging rock and watched the water come down in cold gray sheets and Marisol wrapped both children inside her jacket and looked at the darkness beyond the shelter's edge.

The woman appeared at the border between dry and wet.

Standing at the point where the rock's shelter ended — still, black-dressed, her hair plastered flat by rain that the wind was driving sideways but that did not seem to move her. Her face was in shadow. She was looking at Marisol with a directness that made Marisol understand the look was specifically for her, that no one else in the group was receiving it.

The woman raised her hand. Not a greeting. A direction — back. The way you point when you want someone to understand there is only one choice and they are making the wrong one.

Marisol looked at the group. Beto was on his phone. The others were wrapped in their own exhaustions, eyes down, inward.

She looked back.

The woman was still pointing.

Then a bolt of lightning split the sky to the west and in the white second of it Marisol could see the woman's face — not the face of a stranger, not the generalized face of a vision, but something that pulled at the edges of recognition, that used the specific proportions of the faces Marisol had grown up with, as if whatever was standing in the rain had assembled itself from the available material of her memory and her grief.

The thunder came. When it passed, the rain was only rain.

Marisol sat against the rock wall and felt Rubén's ribs rise and fall under her hands, the steady fact of his breathing, and she thought about what was behind her and what was ahead and she chose, again, what she had already chosen.

She did not go back.

— — —

The Third Night — The River

They reached the river at 1 a.m.

The bank smelled of mud and cold water and something underneath those things — the smell of a place that has received many things and kept them.

"There," Beto said, pointing at the crossing point. "Straight across. Don't stop."

Marisol picked up Rubén and took Camila's hand.

It came from upstream — the voice, the same voice from the desert and the rain, ay, mis hijos, moving against the current. But different now. Closer than it had been either previous night. Close enough that Marisol could hear what she had not been able to hear before: the cadence underneath the words. The particular way the syllable hi lifted before dropping into jos. The extra beat before mis, the breath taken as if the speaker needed one more moment before the word.

Her mother's rhythm. Her own rhythm. The song she had sung to Camila's fear a hundred times.

She stood at the bank and understood something she did not want to understand.

"Mamá," Camila said. She was looking at the water. Her hand had tightened on Marisol's.

"It's okay," Marisol said. "It's okay, mi amor."

She stepped into the river.

The water reached her knee and then her hip and the current was not what Beto had described because it had rained in the mountains four days ago and the river had risen and the pull of it was a fact, impersonal, structural, not evil — just the river being the river, indifferent as rivers always are. She had Rubén on her back and Camila's hand in hers and the crossing was fifteen meters and they were five meters in when Camila went under.

She did not let go of Camila's hand. She went under too.

Rubén's grip on her back was a child's grip, strong in the way children are strong when they are frightened, and then the current found them and the grip was not strong enough and the cold of the water was absolute — not the cold of weather but the cold of depth, of something below the surface that has never been warm — and Marisol pulled at Camila's hand and reached for where Rubén had been and the river moved around her in the dark.

She called their names.

She called them once, clearly, before the water.

And then she called them the only way left to her.

— — —

They found her on a Wednesday morning.

Agent Tomás Reyes drove to the coordinates without hurrying, because hurrying would not change the coordinates. He had worked this sector for eleven years.

The report he filed read: 0814 hrs. Recovery operation, south bank sector seven. Three subjects recovered from shallows. Female, approximately 30. Two minors, female approximately 7, male approximately 4. No documentation. No identification. Transferred to county.

He did not write what he saw. The flowers painted on Camila's sneakers in nail polish — someone's careful work, someone who wanted her to have something pretty. The boy with his knees pulled to his chest the way a seed curls in the ground. The woman with her arms still reaching.

Some things you do not put in a log.

The duty officer assigned them numbers: six hundred and eighty-one, six hundred and eighty-two, six hundred and eighty-three.

Six hundred and eighty-three people had now died crossing this stretch of border.

The number was filed. The shift continued. The river moved.

— — —

One Month Later — Another Group

The new coyote had done this route thirty times.

Eleven people, a different night, the same river. They reached the bank at midnight. The crossing point Beto had used — the water was lower now, the season changing, the conditions what they were supposed to have been a month ago.

"There," the coyote said. "Straight across."

Then they heard it.

Not one voice — two. A woman's voice and underneath it, woven into it, the small sounds of children. Not crying. The sounds children make in sleep, unguarded and soft, as if they are at rest somewhere comfortable. The three voices together formed something that was not a wail and not a lullaby but moved between both — a mother's sound, the most specific and irreducible sound in the world, ay, mis hijos, moving upstream against the current with no regard for the laws of water.

Everyone at the bank went still.

"Animal," the coyote said. "Sound carries —"

"No," said a woman near the back of the group.

Her name was Concepción and she was from Guerrero and her grandmother had told her about La Llorona in the serious tone reserved for things that were true. She had a daughter of seven standing beside her — her granddaughter, technically, her daughter's child — and the girl had stopped moving and was listening to the sound from the river with the full attention of a child who has no defenses against what is true.

"She has children," Concepción said. She said it quietly, to herself and to the sound and to the dark water. "She is telling us."

She picked up her granddaughter and turned away from the river.

The coyote said: it's safe, the water is low, I've done this a hundred times. He had done it thirty. She did not look back. She walked into the desert dark, her granddaughter's legs around her waist, and she did not know where she was going only that it was away from the water and away from the sound of a woman who had not turned back when she should have.

— — —

Yesenia

She was at the shelter when they arrived.

Concepción and her granddaughter came through the door at 3 a.m. — the door of the converted house on the Juárez side that the collective had been running for eight months, the place where people who had turned back came to before they figured out what came next. Marisol's daughter was the one who opened the door.

She was fifteen now. She had grown three inches since September and she had a seriousness about her that was not the seriousness of a teenager but something that had been formed by specific events and would not leave her. She had started coming to the shelter in October because she had nothing else to do with the thing she was carrying and she had understood that doing something was better than doing nothing and this was something.

She opened the door and she did not ask questions. She brought Concepción water and the girl warm food and she sat across from them at the kitchen table while they ate and she looked at the girl the way she looked at all the children who came through this door, which was with a specific attention, the attention of someone looking for something.

Concepción said: "We were at the river. We heard a woman."

Yesenia said nothing.

"She had children with her. You could hear them."

Yesenia looked at her hands on the table. She had been doing that less lately. Looking at them less, doing more. But she looked at them now.

"What did she sound like?" she said.

Concepción was quiet for a moment. Then she described it — the cadence, the particular way the notes fell, the extra breath before mis.

Yesenia nodded.

She stood up and went to the window that faced north toward the river, which was invisible from here but which she knew the direction of the way you know where a scar is without looking. She stood there for a while.

"She's watching the bank," Yesenia said. Not to Concepción — to the window, to the dark, to the river she could not see. "She's still watching."

She turned back to the kitchen. Concepción's granddaughter had fallen asleep over her food, her head on her arms, her breathing slow.

Yesenia covered her with a blanket from the shelf by the door.

She put the kettle on.

She wrote the night's arrivals in the shelter's log: 0310 hrs. Two persons, female 50s and female child 7, turned back from crossing. Safe.

She saved it. She looked at what she had written.

Then she sat down and waited for whoever else the river might send back.

— — —

The Rio Grande / Río Bravo forms a 1,954-mile border between the United States and Mexico. Between 2014 and 2026, the remains of more than 4,100 migrants were recovered along its banks. The number of those never found is unknown.

In Mexican folklore, La Llorona walks the rivers looking for what she lost. Along the border, the story has changed. She is no longer only looking.

She is also warning.

Whether anyone listens depends on who is telling the story, and who is left to tell it.

— — —

02

El Cadejo

The Dogs That Follow

Guatemala City, Zone 18 · February · 2026

The Dogs That Follow

The white one appeared first.

Mateo was thirteen when he noticed it — a dog the color of old bone sitting at the corner of 18 Calle and Avenida Petapa, watching him walk home from school. Not aggressive. Not begging. Just watching, the way dogs sometimes do when they have decided, for reasons of their own, that a particular person is worth their attention.

He threw a rock at it. The dog didn't move.

He told his mother. She set down her dish towel and looked at him with an expression he couldn't read. "What color?" she asked.

"White," he said. "Almost. Like it used to be white."

She picked up the dish towel again. "Don't throw rocks at it," she said. "Don't feed it either. Just leave it alone."

He was thirteen and he wanted an explanation, not instructions. But his mother's family was from Huehuetenango, and she had brought certain knowledges with her to the capital the way you bring seeds — small, dormant, ready to grow in the right conditions. She did not explain. She went back to the dishes.

Mateo left it alone.

— — —

Mateo had grown up reading Zone 18 the way his mother read weather.

Which streets you could walk and which you couldn't. Which colors marked you for attention. The particular quality of silence that fell when certain men turned a corner — not absence of sound but a different kind of sound, everything recalibrating around a new fact in the room.

He knew the volcanoes were visible on clear mornings, Agua and Fuego above the smog, colors that seemed borrowed from somewhere else. He knew the market on Saturdays, the smell of loroco and fresh tortillas, the murals of saints and quetzals on the walls of houses — painted by people who understood that beauty was not a luxury but an argument. We are here. We are not only this.

He also knew that Zone 18 had been Mara territory for twenty years. That this was not a secret. That you learned the whole of it, beauty and threat together, or you didn't survive to learn anything else.

He was fourteen when they first talked to him.

Not the bosses — never the bosses first. It was Chino, who was seventeen and had the easy confidence of someone who has recently acquired something he believes makes him powerful. He fell into step beside Mateo on the way back from the pulpería, a bag of chips in his hand, sharing without being asked.

"You're Doña Carmen's boy," Chino said. It wasn't a question.

"Yes."

"Your father was Rodrigo Suy."

A beat. "He left."

Chino nodded as if this confirmed something he already knew. "We look out for families here," he said. "You know that, right? Nobody bothers Doña Carmen's stall. Nobody has for three years." He offered the chips again. "That's not nothing."

Mateo took the chips. He knew, already, in the way that children who have grown up paying attention know things, that this conversation was a kind of door opening. That taking the chips was a kind of answer. But he was hungry and tired and his school shoes had a hole in the left sole that let in water when it rained, and the chips were there.

He took them.

He didn't see the white dog that night. But the next morning it was back at the corner, and now there was another dog beside it — black, the same size, sitting the same way. Watching.

He stopped walking.

The white dog's tail moved once, slowly. The black one was perfectly still.

Mateo looked at them for a long moment, then kept walking, fast, without looking back. When he reached school he went directly to the bathroom and ran cold water over his wrists until his pulse settled, though he couldn't have explained why his pulse had risen in the first place.

They were dogs. They were just dogs.

— — —

His mother noticed.

Not the dogs — he hadn't told her about the second one — but the chips, the way Chino's name entered the house on Mateo's lips with a casualness that wasn't casual. She was a woman who had raised a child alone in Zone 18 for seven years, which meant she had developed a sensitivity to certain frequencies the way some people develop perfect pitch: not something you could explain, just something you heard before anyone else did.

"Chino Morales," she said.

"He's fine, Mamá."

"He's Mara."

"Everyone here is something."

She put down the spoon she was holding with a precision that meant she was choosing not to throw it. "You are not everyone," she said. "You are my son. You are going to finish school. You are going to—"

"I know," he said. He did know. He had heard this list his whole life, every item on it a stone she was placing between him and a particular future. He didn't tell her the future had started sending representatives. That it shared chips and walked beside you in broad daylight and said your father's name like it was a key it had just found.

He didn't tell her about the dogs.

— — —

By December they were everywhere.

Not always together — sometimes just the white one, at the mouth of an alley, or visible for a second at the far end of a street. Sometimes just the black, which never moved its tail, which watched with an intensity the white one didn't have, something focused in it, something that felt less like observation and more like assessment. And sometimes both, at the same distance, flanking him at exactly the width of a narrow doorway.

He had stopped throwing rocks. He had stopped telling himself they were just dogs.

Chino had introduced him to a man named Pulga, who was twenty-two and smelled of cigarettes and something chemical that Mateo recognized from the older boys at school without being able to name it. Pulga had given him small jobs — not the obvious ones, not yet. Carrying packages he wasn't supposed to open. Waiting on a corner at a specific time and walking away at another specific time. Being present, which was itself a kind of message: we have people everywhere, even the young ones, even the ones still in school.

He was paid in cash. He put it in an envelope under his mattress and told himself it was for his mother's stall, for the new grill she needed, for the shoes with a solid sole. This was mostly true. The part that wasn't true he didn't examine.

One night in December, walking back from a corner he'd been told to stand on, he stopped because both dogs were blocking the path. Not aggressively — they weren't growling, weren't advancing. Just sitting in the middle of the narrow alley between two houses, side by side, looking at him.

The white one and the black one.

He stood there for a long moment. The alley smelled of woodsmoke and sewage and the particular cold of

December in the capital, which is not the cold of mountains but something damper, closer, that gets into your clothes and stays.

"Move," he said.

Neither dog moved.

"Muévanse." He took a step forward. The white dog's ears went back — not in aggression but in something that looked almost like distress. The black one still hadn't moved at all. It seemed to him, standing in the cold alley at nine at night, that the black dog wasn't watching him the way the white one was. The white one watched him the way his mother watched him. The black one watched him the way Pulga watched him.

He went around them, pressing against the wall. They let him pass. He did not look back.

— — —

Señora Carmen — Zone 18, January

She found the envelope.

She hadn't been looking for it. She'd been changing his sheets — he was fifteen now, old enough to do it himself, but she still did it when he was at school because it was one of the few things she could still do for him that he hadn't yet learned to refuse. The envelope was under the mattress, thin and folded, and she opened it with hands that had already decided what they were going to find.

Four hundred quetzales.

She sat on his bed for a long time. Outside, the neighborhood made its noises — the neighbors' television, a motorcycle somewhere below, a dog barking twice and then going quiet. Ordinary sounds. The sounds of a place that had learned to be ordinary about extraordinary things.

She knew what the money was. She had grown up here. She had watched the same current take boys the way a river takes branches — not all at once, not dramatically, just a gradual movement in a direction you don't notice until it's too late to swim back.

She thought about her mother, who had told her about el Cadejo. Two dogs, she'd said. The white one walks with the good ones. The black one walks with the ones who are choosing badly. If you see both, her mother had told her, it means the soul is still deciding. That is the most dangerous time. That is when you fight hardest.

Señora Carmen put the money back in the envelope and the envelope back under the mattress. Then she went to the kitchen and began making pepián, because when she didn't know what else to do she cooked, and the grinding of seeds and the smell of charred tomatoes was the closest thing she had to prayer.

She would talk to him tonight. She would find the words.

She had been trying to find the words for two years. She was not sure there were words equal to what the street offered — the money, the belonging, the dangerous intoxication of being seen. She was one woman in a kitchen making pepián. She was not nothing. But she was also not enough, and she had known that for a long time, and the knowing of it was a stone she carried so constantly she had stopped noticing the weight.

The seeds ground down. The kitchen filled with smoke and the smell of something old and true.

She prayed anyway, wordlessly, to whatever was listening.

— — —

They gave him the gun in February.

Not Chino — Chino had moved up, moved out, was somewhere in Zone 5 now, or so Mateo had heard. It was Pulga, and it happened the way Mateo had always known, in the part of himself he didn't examine, that it would happen: simply, matter-of-factly, the way you hand someone a tool when you've decided they're ready to use it.

"There's a man," Pulga said. "He owes. He knows he owes. He just needs reminding."

The gun was a .38, heavier than Mateo had expected. He had touched guns before — you couldn't grow up in Zone 18 without that — but this one was different because it had his fingerprints on it now, and Pulga was watching him hold it with an expression that was also a test.

"I'm not—" Mateo started.

"You're not shooting anyone," Pulga said. "You're just showing. He sees the gun, he pays. That's all." He smiled. "You've been carrying packages for five months. This is just a different package."

Mateo looked at the gun.

He thought about his mother's stall. He thought about Chino saying we look out for families here. He thought about the cold alley and the two dogs and the way the white one's ears had gone back, and he thought about a conversation he'd had with his grandmother on the phone last Easter, when she'd asked him how school was going and he'd said fine and she'd said your mother says you're very smart and he hadn't known what to do with that so he'd just said yes, Abuela and moved on.

"Tonight," Pulga said. "Eleven. I'll walk with you the first time."

Mateo put the gun in his waistband. He felt it there, warm from Pulga's hand, pressing against the small of his back like a second spine.

— — —

He saw them outside his building.

Both of them. Under the single working streetlight at the end of the block, sitting at the edge of where the light fell into dark, equidistant from the lamp, from each other, from him. White and black. Perfectly still.

He stopped walking.

Pulga was beside him. "What?" Pulga said, following his gaze. "What are you looking at?"

Mateo looked at Pulga. "The dogs," he said.

Pulga looked at the streetlight, at the dark beyond it. "What dogs?"

A long silence. The neighborhood breathed around them — television noise, a baby somewhere, music from a house up the hill, the thin incessant sound of traffic on the Avenida.

"Never mind," Mateo said.

The white dog stood up. Just the white one — the black stayed sitting. It took three steps toward him and stopped. Its tail was moving, low and slow, the way a tail moves when a dog is uncertain, when it wants something it doesn't know how to ask for.

Pulga checked his phone. "Vámonos. He leaves after midnight."

Mateo stood there. The gun at his back. Pulga beside him. His mother's building two floors above. The white dog three meters away, looking at him with an expression that was not a dog's expression, that was something older and more specific — something that knew his name and his grandmother's name and the exact amount of money in the envelope under his mattress.

He thought: my mother is upstairs.

He thought: she made pepián last night and didn't ask me anything.

He thought: she knows.

The white dog took one more step.

"I'm not going," Mateo said.

Pulga turned. "What?"

"I'm not going." He reached behind his back and held out the gun. His hand was shaking. He was aware of the shaking and could not stop it and decided not to try. "I'm not doing this."

Pulga looked at the gun. Looked at Mateo. Something shifted in his face — the easy confidence compressing into something harder and colder, something that had been underneath it all along.

"You think about what you're saying," Pulga said quietly.

"I have." He kept his hand out. Steady now, surprisingly. "Take it."

A long moment. The streetlight buzzed. Somewhere up the hill the music changed.

Pulga took the gun.

He held it at his side and looked at Mateo for a long time. Not with anger — anger would have been easier. With the flat, patient expression of someone making a calculation.

"You have a mother," Pulga said. "Doña Carmen. The stall on the corner." He paused. "Nice woman."

He didn't say anything else. He didn't have to.

His footsteps faded down the block. Turned a corner. Gone.

Mateo stood alone under the light.

He looked at where the dogs had been.

The black dog was gone.

The white one was still there — close now, close enough that he could have touched it. It looked up at him and its eyes held the streetlight in them like two small flames. Then it turned and walked into the dark.

He didn't watch it go. He was already running.

— — —

He told his mother in four sentences.

She was at the kitchen table, which meant she had been waiting, which meant she already knew the shape of it even if not the details. He told her about Pulga. About the gun. About what Pulga had said before he left.

She was quiet for three seconds. Then she stood up.

"How long do we have?"

"I don't know. Tonight. Maybe."

She nodded once. She did not cry. She went to the bedroom and he heard the sound of the closet opening, the particular drag of the bag she kept on the top shelf — the one she had told him, years ago, was for emergencies, the one he had thought was for earthquakes, for floods, for the kinds of disasters that had names and warning systems.

Not for this. And also, always, for this.

They packed in forty minutes. Two bags. Documents in the inside pocket of her coat. The money from under his mattress — all of it. A photograph of his grandmother that she took from the wall without looking at it, tucking it between two shirts. He took nothing except his school bag with his textbooks still inside, because he didn't know what else to take and the textbooks were there and they were his and he was fifteen years old and he didn't know how to choose what to save of a life.

At 1 a.m. they slipped out through the building's back entrance, down the service stairs, through the courtyard where Señor Alvarado's dog usually barked at everything.

The dog didn't bark.

It was watching the front entrance. Head low. Growling at something in the street that Mateo couldn't see from the courtyard.

He pulled his mother's arm. They went the other way.

— — —

The bus to Huehuetenango left at 4 a.m. from the terminal in Zone 4. They got there at 2:30 and sat in the plastic chairs under the fluorescent lights and did not speak. His mother had her bag on her lap and both hands on it. Mateo watched the entrance.

At 3:15 his phone buzzed.

A number he didn't recognize. No message. Just the call, which he let ring out, and then the notification: missed call.

Then a second buzz. A photo.

Their front door. The door of their apartment in Zone 18. Taken from the hallway, close up, timestamped eleven minutes ago.

He showed his mother. She looked at it. She put her hand over his phone screen so she didn't have to see it anymore.

"Don't answer," she said.

He wasn't going to answer.

The bus came. They got on. It pulled out of the terminal into the dark city, through zones he knew and zones he didn't, toward the western highway and the mountains and whatever came next, which he couldn't see and couldn't plan for and could only move toward because the alternative was to stop moving.

He looked out the window as the city thinned around them.

At the last corner before the highway — under a streetlight at the edge of Zone 18's boundary, where the pavement cracked and the houses gave way to scrubland — a dog sat watching the bus pass.

Black.

Still.

Its eyes caught the headlights for just a moment and threw them back: two cold points of light in the dark.

Then the bus turned, and the city was behind them, and there was only the road and the mountains and the long dark before morning.

Mateo faced forward.

He did not look back again.

— — —

Zone 18 in Guatemala City has one of the highest homicide rates in the Western Hemisphere. The Mara Salvatrucha and Barrio 18 gangs have controlled large sections of the neighborhood for over two decades. The average age of gang recruitment in Guatemala is fourteen. According to UNICEF, more than 40% of recruits are children.

El Cadejo is one of the most widely shared legends in Central America, appearing in Guatemala, El Salvador, Honduras, and Mexico. The white Cadejo is a protector; the black, a corruptor. To see both simultaneously is considered a sign that a person stands at a crossroads — that their fate has not yet been written.

— — —

03

La Viuda

The Widow's Rate

Panama City, Casco Viejo · A Saturday in October · 2026

The Widow's Rate

The celebration started at nine.

There were twelve of them at the long table in the private room at Maito — the firm's senior partners and their guests, bottles of Clase Azul going around, the particular looseness that comes after a very large wire transfer clears. Rodrigo Salcedo sat at the head of the table the way he always sat at the head of things: leaning back, one arm over the chair beside him, talking without needing to raise his voice because rooms reorganized themselves around his volume.

He was forty-four years old. He had a wife in Punta Pacífica and a daughter at the American School and a second apartment in Marbella that neither of them knew about. He had, in the last eleven years, structured the financial arrangements of three former heads of state, one sitting vice president, seven major narcotics organizations, and a Swiss commodities firm whose activities he had made it his business not to understand too precisely. He had never been charged with anything. He had never even been seriously investigated, because the people who might have investigated him had, in several cases, been clients.

Tonight they were celebrating the successful restructuring of a Venezuelan oil executive's assets — two hundred and forty million dollars moved through a chain of shell companies across four jurisdictions and deposited, clean and untraceable, into accounts that officially belonged to a Panamanian real estate development company that officially employed eleven people and officially had no connection to anyone at this table.

Rodrigo raised his glass.

"To complexity," he said.

Everyone drank.

— — —

He noticed her at the bar when the dinner broke up and the partners moved to the adjacent lounge.

She was sitting alone, which was the first thing. Not in the way women sit alone at bars when they want company — that has a particular posture, an orientation toward the room, a readiness. She was sitting with her back to most of the lounge, a glass of red wine barely touched in front of her, looking at the far wall with the focused inattention of someone who has a great deal on their mind.

She was wearing black. Not fashionable black — the specific black of mourning, a dress that had been chosen for grief and not for evenings out, slightly wrong for the room in a way that made her more visible rather than less.

Rodrigo had built his career on reading rooms and the people in them. He read her in thirty seconds: recently widowed, money, out of her depth in grief, the kind of woman who has spent a life being managed and is now, for the first time, managing alone. An evening's distraction, nothing more.

He took his drink and crossed the room.

"You look like someone who's had a difficult week," he said.

She turned. Her face was striking — dark eyes, a stillness in her features that wasn't quite calm, something underneath it that he categorized as grief and moved on. "Difficult year," she said. Her accent was Panamanian. Old money — the vowels of someone who had grown up with domestic staff and European educations.

"I'm sorry for your loss," he said, though he didn't know what the loss was. It was a useful phrase. It covered most situations.

"Are you?" she said. Not challenging — genuinely curious, as if she were collecting data.

He sat down. She let him. He signaled the bartender.

Her name, she told him, was Isabel. Her husband had died eight months ago. A heart attack, she said, though something in the way she said it — a slight pause before the words, a flatness, the tone of a person reciting something they have said many times and have stopped believing — made him file the detail without examining it. He had learned, over many years, that the stories people told about their dead were rarely the whole story, and it was usually more useful to listen for the gaps than the words.

They talked for an hour. She was intelligent — more than he'd expected, more than most people he spent time with, which was a quality he recognized with the slight wariness of a man who is used to being the smartest person present. She asked questions that seemed simple and weren't. She had a way of going quiet at the end of his answers, a pause that lasted exactly long enough to make him want to keep talking, to fill the silence with more than he'd intended to give.

He found himself telling her about the restructuring. Not the details — never the details, not even after three drinks — but the shape of it, the elegance of what they'd accomplished, the particular pleasure of a problem solved at sufficient scale that it became, in his view, almost architectural. He was proud of his work. He rarely got to express this directly.

She listened. The dark eyes didn't move from his face.

"Doesn't it bother you?" she asked. "The source."

"I'm a lawyer," he said. "I structure arrangements. What goes into the structure is someone else's concern."

"Of course," she said. And smiled for the first time — a small, precise smile that he couldn't quite read, which was unusual, which he should perhaps have paid more attention to.

He paid the bill. She accepted his card for her wine without comment. He asked if she'd like to continue the evening somewhere else, and she tilted her head and looked at him with an expression that was yes without being yes, which was an answer he had encountered before and always found encouraging.

They walked out into the Casco Viejo night.

— — —

Isabel — Casco Viejo, eight months earlier

The night she found Carlos's records, she sat at the kitchen table until 4 a.m.

He had been meticulous. Two years of copies — client files, wire transfers, correspondence, internal memos written in the careful euphemisms of men who understand that language is also a kind of shell company. He had assembled everything, annotated it, stored it in three locations. Then died of a heart attack at fifty-one, at his desk, alone in the office at 11 p.m. on a Tuesday.

She had thought he was working late. He had been working late for two years. He had been working on this.

The client whose name appeared most often was a Venezuelan named Armando Vega. She had met Vega once, at a dinner. A big man, warm handshake, the easy manner of someone accustomed to being liked. She had told Carlos on the way home that she found him charming. Carlos had said nothing.

She understood now why.

The cargo manifests were in the third folder. She read them once, then set them face-down on the table, then picked them up and read them again, because the first time she had read them hoping she was wrong.

She was not wrong.

Carlos had known for two years what was moving on Vega's vessels. Had structured the arrangements, built the companies, received the fees. Had spent two years afraid, protecting her from it, unable to find the way out. And then died, and left her the records, and the decision.

She made the decision that night.

It took eight months to execute. She was meticulous too — she had learned that from him, among other things. She found the right contact at the Fiscalía. The right journalist at the International Consortium of Investigative Journalists — ICIJ. The right sequence. She dressed in the black she had worn since the funeral. She went to Maito on the night she knew the firm would be celebrating.

She had done her research. She knew who Rodrigo Salcedo was. She knew his table, his habits, his particular appetite for women who appeared to need managing.

She ordered red wine and waited.

— — —

Rodrigo had an apartment three blocks from Maito — not the one in Marbella, the one his wife knew about as an investment property. The neighborhood had appreciated forty percent in seven years, which was the fact about Casco Viejo he found most interesting. The cobblestones and ruins and bougainvillea were fine, were useful for the premium they added to the per-square-meter price, were things he mentioned when he needed to explain why he spent so much time here. He had walked this route many times. He knew it the way he knew the structure of a well-crafted shell company: from the outside, clean and unremarkable; from the inside, a series of useful compartments.

Isabel walked beside him.

She moved through Casco Viejo with a familiarity that slightly surprised him — she knew to step around the loose cobblestone on Avenida Central, she took the corner at Calle 3 without hesitation, she looked at the ruins along the waterfront not with the curious attention of a tourist but with the proprietary awareness of someone who has walked here at night many times before.

"You know this neighborhood," he said.

"I know it well," she said.

They passed a cat sleeping on a stone wall. They passed the old church with its collapsed roof open to the sky, the stars visible through the gap. Rodrigo was talking — he couldn't have said what about, something about the architecture, the history, the plans for the restoration that had been announced and delayed and announced again. He liked to talk about history. It gave a context to his work that he found settling.

Isabel let him talk. She was looking at the waterfront, at the dark water of the bay, which at this hour was perfectly still and reflected the lights of the city back at itself in wavering columns.

"My husband used to walk here," she said.

"Tell me about him."

Another pause. Longer this time. She turned from the water and looked at Rodrigo directly, the first time she had looked at him with that full attention rather than the sideways listening she'd done all evening.

"He was a careful man," she said. "Methodical. He kept records of everything." She paused. "He worked with a firm like yours. Not yours exactly. But like it." Another pause. "He had a client he was frightened of. He had been frightened for two years, and I hadn't known — he protected me from it. And then one day he had a heart attack, and then he was dead, and then I found the records."

Rodrigo was quiet.

"What did you do with them?" he said. His voice had changed. He couldn't help that.

"I've been deciding," she said simply.

They had stopped walking. They were at the edge of the waterfront promenade, the bay before them, the old city rising behind. The water was very still. Somewhere out in the bay a boat light blinked slowly.

He looked at her. The black dress. The barely-touched wine. The questions that seemed simple and weren't.

A lawyer, after all. He should have read her better.

"What do you want?" he said.

She reached into her bag and placed a USB drive on the stone railing between them. It was small and ordinary, a cheap blue plastic casing, the kind you bought at a pharmacy. She held it there with one finger on top of it the way you hold something you might take back.

"What's on that?" he said, though he suspected.

"Your firm's work for the Venezuelan. And six others." She paused. "My husband was meticulous. He kept copies of everything, including things that were never meant to be copied." She looked at him. "The United Nations Office on Drugs and Crime would find it very interesting. So would ICIJ. You know what they did with the last batch."

He did know. He had spent three months watching colleagues lose everything, watching names he recognized scroll across every news site in the world, and he had sat in his office and been grateful, for the first time, that he had been careful enough to use other people's names on the documents.

"What do you want?" he said again.

"To know something," she said. "Before I decide."

"Know what?"

She looked at him steadily. "Whether you knew what the money was for. Not the structure. Not the jurisdictions. The money itself — the Venezuelan oil executive, the cargo he was moving. Whether you knew what was in it."

A long silence. The water lapped at the stones below. The city breathed around them.

Rodrigo was not a man who told the truth when lying was available. He had built his entire career on the proposition that truth was an instrument, to be deployed when useful and withheld when not. He opened his mouth.

And found, with a surprise that was also a kind of physical sensation, that he could not lie to her.

Not the way he couldn't lie to a judge — not fear. Something else. Her eyes on him in the dark, the specific quality of her attention, the way she was waiting, which was not the way people wait when they're expecting an answer but the way people wait when they already know the answer and are giving you the chance to say it yourself.

He had known what was in it.

He had always known. He had constructed very carefully the architecture of not-knowing — the layers of legal language and corporate structure that let him say, truthfully, that he had never been told, never officially informed, never given documentation that would constitute legal knowledge. But underneath that architecture, in the room he never went into, the thing had always been there. Human cargo. The Venezuelan's real business, the thing the oil was cover for, the thing that moved on the same vessels, in the same containers, through the same channels he had so elegantly structured.

He had known. He had chosen, very deliberately, not to know.

"Yes," he said.

Isabel looked at him for a moment. Then she picked up the USB drive and put it back in her bag.

"Then we're done," she said.

"What does that mean?"

She was already walking — not back toward Maito, not toward anywhere he recognized. Toward the water, along the promenade, away from the lights.

"Isabel —"

She didn't turn.

"What are you going to do with it?" he called.

She stopped. Didn't turn. Her voice came back to him over the water, steady and clear in the 2 a.m. silence.

"What I should have done eight months ago," she said. "When I found out what he'd done. And what he'd helped do." A pause. "And what it cost."

She walked on. The dark took her in, the particular dark of the waterfront in the old city, which is not an absence of light but a presence of something older.

He stood at the railing for a long time.

— — —

They froze his accounts on a Thursday.

He was in the office when it happened — a Thursday afternoon in the ordinary course of things, sun through the floor-to-ceiling windows, his assistant bringing coffee, the city laid out below him in the particular clarity of Panama's dry season. His phone buzzed. Then his computer. Then his assistant appeared in the doorway with an expression he had never seen on her face before and said: "There are men from the Fiscalía in reception."

Three other partners were arrested the same day. One fled. Two cooperated immediately. Rodrigo's own lawyer — he had a personal lawyer, of course, everyone in his position did — arrived within the hour and said the word ICIJ and collaboration and documentation and chain of custody in a tone that Rodrigo recognized as the tone lawyers used when they were trying to prepare you for something they already knew you weren't prepared for.

The documentation was meticulous. It had been assembled over two years, copied carefully, stored in multiple locations, cross-referenced and annotated in a hand that the Fiscalía's experts identified as belonging to one Carlos Valentín Sosa, deceased, formerly a senior associate of a competing firm, cause of death recorded as cardiac arrest.

His wife had signed the handover agreement three weeks ago.

— — —

Rodrigo's lawyer negotiated a deal. It took eight months and cost everything that wasn't already frozen — suspended sentence, revoked license, a name appearing in fourteen languages on the ICIJ's public database. His apartment in Marbella was seized. His wife filed for divorce the week the story broke. His daughter stopped returning his calls.

He gave interviews in which he described the woman at the bar as a honeytrap. A setup. The calculated seduction of a man who had been drinking. He used words like targeted and entrapped and agenda and spoke of his own culpability in careful, limited terms, the way a man speaks when he has been coached on exactly how much to admit.

The interviews stopped after the daughter gave one of her own.

— — —

He went back to Casco Viejo on a Tuesday night in November, eleven months after he had first walked out of Maito with a woman in black beside him. He drove himself — no driver anymore, no assistant, no one who needed to know where he was going. He parked on Avenida Central and walked the route he had walked before, past the old church with its collapsed roof, past the cat's wall which was empty now, to the promenade at the edge of the bay.

The water was still. The same boat light blinked somewhere in the dark.

He stood at the railing where he had stood with her. He put his hands on the stone, which was cold, which had been cold for longer than he had been alive. He looked at the water, which reflected the city back at itself in wavering columns — all that light, all that commerce, all that careful structure, shimmering and impermanent on the surface of something very old and very dark.

He had told one truth in his life.

He stood there for a long time.

In the morning, a street cleaner found a jacket folded over the railing. In one pocket, a phone with a cracked screen, battery dead. In the other, a USB drive in a cheap blue plastic casing.

The police report noted the time. It noted the location. It noted the absence of any other evidence, the unbroken surface of the water, the way the bay gives nothing back.

— — —

The Panama Papers, leaked in 2016, exposed 11.5 million documents from the Panamanian law firm Mossack Fonseca. The files revealed how the firm helped clients — including heads of state, oligarchs, and convicted criminals — hide assets in shell companies across multiple jurisdictions. 143 politicians from more than 50 countries were implicated. The leak was the largest in journalistic history at the time.

La Viuda — The Widow — is a spirit from Central American, South American, and Caribbean folklore, reported across Panama, Colombia, and Guatemala. She appears at night as a beautiful woman in mourning dress, targeting men who have done wrong. Those she encounters rarely speak of it afterward.

— — —

04

La Sayona

What She Leaves Behind

Caracas, Torre Sindical · October to November · 2026

What She Leaves Behind

The blackouts came every day now.

In the Torre Sindical — twenty-two floors of crumbling concrete in the heart of Caracas, home to nine hundred people who had moved in when the government stopped paying attention to who was moving in — the blackouts lasted anywhere from two hours to two days. You could not predict them. You could only prepare: candles, water in every container that would hold it, a flashlight by the bed, the particular mental adjustment of a person who has learned not to be surprised by the dark.

Inspector Graciela Pino had lived on the fourteenth floor for six years. She knew the building's sounds the way a doctor knows a patient's breathing — the groan of the elevator that still worked on alternate days, the specific acoustics of the stairwell that carried conversations three floors, the 3 a.m. quiet that was different from the 11 p.m. quiet in ways she could feel before she could name them.

She knew the building's rhythms.

Which was how she knew that the man in 9B had not left his apartment in eleven days.

— — —

His name was Freddy Useche. Thirty-eight, worked — or had worked — dispatch for a trucking company in Petare. She had interviewed him twice in the last two months, both times in connection with a case she was not officially allowed to be working: the disappearance of a woman named Luisa Moreno, thirty-three, who had lived in 11C until seven weeks ago when she had not come home from a shift at the pharmacy on Avenida Libertador.

Freddy had been Luisa's boyfriend.

The interviews had yielded nothing usable. He was a man who understood how to be interviewed — what to offer, what to withhold, how to arrange his face into the appropriate configurations of grief and confusion. He had cried in the second interview, which in Graciela's experience meant nothing either way. She had been doing this for eleven years. She had stopped reading tears as evidence of anything except the presence of tears.

What she had taken from those interviews was something that couldn't go in a report: the specific quality of his stillness when she mentioned Luisa's name. Not the stillness of grief, which collapses inward. The other kind — the stillness of a man holding something in place.

She had three other open cases with the same shape. All women. All last seen in the company of men who knew how to be interviewed. All in buildings in this part of Caracas where the blackouts were long and the stairwells were dark and the particular quality of a woman's scream could be, if you chose, mistaken for the building settling.

— — —

The first report came from the eighth floor.

A woman named Doris, sixties, who sold arepas from a cart in the lobby and saw everything and was the closest thing the Torre Sindical had to an official record-keeper. She came to Graciela's door at 7 a.m. on a Wednesday, before the building fully woke, and told her what she'd seen three weeks ago now: a woman, during a blackout, in the stairwell between floors eight and nine.

"What did she look like?" Graciela said.

Doris thought about it. "Beautiful," she said. "But wrong."

"Wrong how?"

"The way she moved. Like she knew where she was going in the dark." Doris paused. "She was in black. Mourning black. An old dress, not for now." Another pause. "I called to her. She didn't answer. She went up."

"To nine."

Doris looked at her. "To nine."

"Has she come back?"

Doris wrapped both hands around her coffee cup. "Every night," she said. "Every blackout, she goes up. She does not come back down." She paused. "And every night — I hear him."

"Hear what?"

Doris was quiet for a moment. "At first, crying. The way men cry when they think no one can hear." She set down the cup. "Now it is different. Now it is something worse than crying. Now it is a man asking for something to stop."

— — —

Freddy — Torre Sindical, Week One

The first night she appeared, he told himself it was the drink.

He had been drinking since noon — not heavily, he was not a man who got sloppy, but steadily, with purpose, because the thing that had been sitting in his chest since he did what he did was easiest to manage at a particular level of numbness, and he had become very skilled at maintaining that level.

The blackout came at 9 p.m. He lit the candle. He sat at the kitchen table. The building made its adjustment noises.

At 9:40, something outside his door.

Not a knock. Not footsteps. A presence — the way air pressure changes when a body occupies space on the other side of a wall. The way a room becomes slightly less empty even through doors.

He sat very still.

I know you're there, he said. His voice was steady. He was proud of that.

Nothing.

He went to the door. Opened it. The stairwell was dark — the emergency light on the ninth floor had failed months ago. He stood in the doorway with the candle behind him throwing his shadow into the dark.

She was at the far end of the landing. Still. In black — an old dress, wrong for this building, wrong for this century. Her face in shadow. Not moving.

He stared.

The candle sputtered. When it steadied, the landing was empty.

He told himself it was the drink. He told himself this very firmly, standing in the dark doorway, and went back inside and did not sleep.

— — —

Freddy — Torre Sindical, Week Two

She was there every night now.

Not always in the stairwell. Sometimes he felt her before the blackout — a drop in the apartment's temperature, a stillness in the air that had nothing to do with the weather. She had been in his apartment once, he was almost certain. He had woken at 2 a.m. to find the candle on the kitchen table lit, though he had not lit it, and the window open, though he had sealed it.

He had not sealed the window against the smell anymore. He no longer noticed the smell.

He had stopped eating with any regularity. He had stopped answering his phone. He had been called in twice by his supervisor and had given explanations that he could tell, even as he said them, were not convincing. The careful presentation he had always maintained — the groomed appearance, the steady voice, the appropriate expressions — was getting harder to sustain. Things were showing through the surface that he had always kept below it.

The fifth night of the second week, she knocked.

Not the presence — an actual knock. Three times, measured, the way a person knocks when they are patient and have decided that patience is the correct instrument.

He pressed himself against the wall opposite the door and did not move until morning.

In the morning he found, slipped under the door, a single photograph. He did not know how it had gotten there. It was a photograph of Luisa — not one he had taken, not one from any source he could identify. She was laughing at something outside the frame. She was wearing the yellow dress she had worn the first time he told her he loved her.

He sat on the kitchen floor for a very long time with the photograph in his hands.

That night, when the blackout came, he did not light the candle. He sat in the total dark and waited and when the knock came — three times, measured, patient — he put his hands over his ears.

It did not help.

— — —

Freddy — Torre Sindical, Week Three

He had not slept in four days.

Every time he closed his eyes she was there — not as a vision, not as a dream, but as a presence behind his eyelids, the way an image burns into your retinas when you look at something too bright and then close your eyes and still see it. He could not explain this to anyone. He could not explain any of it.

He had tried leaving the apartment on the ninth day. Got as far as the stairwell. The emergency light on the ninth floor had been dark for months — but that night there was a glow on the landing, faint and sourceless, and in it he could see her at the bottom of the stairs, looking up at him.

He went back inside. He did not try again.

The knock came every night now without the blackout. Day or night, power on or off, 3 a.m. or noon — three knocks, measured, patient. Sometimes a long silence and then three more. Sometimes just the three, then nothing until he had almost convinced himself it was over, and then three more.

He began to talk to her through the door.

Not coherently — he was past coherent. He said Luisa's name. He said I know and I'm sorry and please and please and please, and none of it changed anything, and the knock came again, and he understood in the way you understand things when you have gone past the point of self-deception that this was not going to stop.

It was not going to stop.

On the eleventh day he sat at the kitchen table and thought about what kind of men came to ends like this and decided that he knew the answer and that the answer was men like him, and this was the thought he was having when Graciela knocked on his door.

— — —

She had not planned to come that morning. She had been passing through the ninth floor on her way to interview a witness on eleven when she heard it — a sound from 9B that was not crying, not anymore, that was something underneath crying, a man making sounds that had given up the structure of language.

She knocked.

The sounds stopped.

She knocked again.

Footsteps. Slow, the footsteps of a person who is moving because they have decided they no longer care about the outcome of moving. The door opened.

Freddy Useche looked at her from the other side of it.

Graciela had interviewed men in many conditions over eleven years — arrested, drunk, in grief, in shock, in the particular blankness of someone who has decided to stop feeling. She had never seen what she saw now. He was not in any of those conditions. He was in a condition she did not have a name for. A man who has been taken apart piece by piece and is still technically standing only because his body has not yet received the instruction to fall.

"Come in," he said. His voice was the voice of someone who learned the phrase once and is now just producing the sounds.

She came in. The apartment was dark — curtains drawn, candles everywhere, guttered and cold, the detritus of eleven days of not leaving. The photograph was on the kitchen table. She looked at it and looked away.

She did not sit. She stood in the middle of the room and looked at him.

"Make it stop," he said.

"Tell me where she is."

Something moved in his face — not resistance, there was no resistance left, just the last twitch of a reflex that had forgotten what it was protecting. "I can't," he said. And then: "I can't do this anymore. Please. Please make it stop."

"Where is Luisa."

He told her. He told her in the collapsed, half-language of a man who has passed through exhaustion into somewhere beyond it — the location, the date, what he had done with what remained. She wrote it down. Her handwriting was very steady. She had learned steadiness over eleven years, in rooms like this, hearing things like this, writing them down.

When he finished he was on the floor. She did not remember him getting there. He was simply on the floor with his back against the kitchen cabinets and his hands in his lap and his eyes at a point on the middle distance that was not anything in the room.

"Please," he said. Quietly. "I'll confess to anything. I'll sign anything. Just make it stop."

She looked at him for a long moment.

She looked at the photograph on the kitchen table. Luisa laughing at something outside the frame, wearing the yellow dress.

She looked at the files in her bag — not just Luisa, the three others, the other men in other buildings who had known how to be interviewed. She thought about the system she had worked inside for eleven years. The cases that went nowhere. The prosecutors who declined. The judges who reduced. The men who walked and were seen the following week in the same stairwells, the same buildings, the same darkness.

She thought about Freddy Useche's face in those first two interviews. The careful performance. The precise tears.

She closed her notebook.

"I don't know what you're talking about," she said.

He looked up at her.

"I came to ask you some follow-up questions about Luisa Moreno," she said. "You weren't able to help me. I'm sorry to have disturbed you." She picked up her bag. She walked to the door. She opened it.

"Wait —" His voice cracked. "Wait. Please. Please, you have to —"

"Get some rest," she said. "You look unwell."

She closed the door behind her.

— — —

She found Luisa in three days. The location was precise — Freddy had been very precise, by the end, when precision was all he had left to offer. She filed the recovery report. She filed the reports for the other three cases, anonymously sourced, location only, no name attached to the information. She was a careful woman. She knew how to build a document that told you exactly what you needed to know and nothing you didn't.

Four families received calls.

Doris, when Graciela stopped at her cart the morning after, poured two cups of coffee without being asked.

"The woman in black," Graciela said. "Is she still going up?"

Doris looked at her for a moment. "Every night," she said. "Every blackout."

Graciela nodded. She drank her coffee. Outside, the building made its sounds — nine hundred lives arranged around each other in the dark, all the ordinary noise of people getting through another day.

"Good," she said.

She finished the coffee and went to work.

— — —

Eleven months later, a patrol officer filed an incident report for apartment 9B, Torre Sindical. Tenant reported hearing a woman's voice in the corridor every evening, sometimes during daylight hours. Tenant appeared severely malnourished, disoriented, unable to provide a coherent account of events. Tenant had not left the building in eleven months. Neighbors confirmed.

The officer noted that the tenant kept saying one word, over and over, when asked about the voice.

Por favor. Please.

The officer filed the report. It went, as most things did, nowhere.

In the stairwell between floors eight and nine, the emergency light continued not to work. The building continued to be dark between those floors, at all hours, regardless of the state of the electrical grid.

No one on the ninth floor complained.

— — —

Venezuela has one of the highest rates of femicide in Latin America. Between 2016 and 2023, over 3,000 women were killed by intimate partners — a figure human rights organizations believe to be significantly undercounted due to systematic failures in reporting and investigation. In cases where charges are filed, conviction rates remain below 20%.

La Sayona is a spirit of vengeance from Venezuelan and Colombian folklore. She appears to men who have done wrong and does not leave until she has taken what she came for. What exactly she takes varies, depending on who is telling the story.

No one agrees on whether she is finished when the man is finished, or whether she continues regardless.

— — —

05

El Silbón

The Same Bones

Los Llanos, Colombia-Venezuela · A night in March · 2026

The Same Bones

The Llanos at night have no edges.

No walls, no treeline, no horizon you can fix a point on and say: there, that is where the dark ends. The grassland runs flat in every direction until it becomes sky, and the sky runs flat above it until it becomes grass, and a man walking in it at night without landmarks is not lost in any direction — he is lost in all of them equally.

There were two men walking.

One had a gun. The other had his hands tied behind his back with electrical cord, walking in front, the gun at his spine.

The one with the gun wore a faded olive green shirt, the kind that had been standard issue for the FARC for forty years, worn now out of habit rather than supply. His name was Mauricio. He had been doing this work for nine years.

The one walking in front wore a jacket with a small Colombian flag stitched to the left shoulder — the patch of the Autodefensas Gaitanistas, the paramilitary bloc that controlled the corridor between the Ariari River and the Venezuelan border. His name was Camilo. He had been doing this work for eleven.

"Left," Mauricio said.

"Left takes us away from —"

"Left."

They turned left.

— — —

"You don't know where we are."

"I know exactly where we are."

"Then why have we passed that same palm three times?"

Silence. The wind moved through the grass — the sound the Llanos made instead of silence, a slow permanent brushing, like something enormous breathing.

"Palms look alike at night."

"That one has a crack in the trunk. Lightning. I noticed it the first time."

"Walk."

"You captured me to guide you to the site. I cannot guide you if you keep turning me left."

The gun pressed harder. "You think I won't use this."

"I think you need me alive until we get there. After that I have no opinion."

A pause. "After that you confess to what your people did in this corridor and you sign a statement for the prosecutor."

Camilo almost laughed. "The same prosecutor who spent ten years charging guerrilla members while every mass grave your organization dug in this corridor went uninvestigated? That prosecutor?"

The gun was still. Then: "Walk."

— — —

"Your people started because the land was stolen," Camilo said. "That is what you tell yourselves."

"It's not what we tell ourselves. It's what happened." Mauricio's voice was steady. "1964. The government sent the army to Marquetalia to destroy a community of farmers who had organized themselves to survive. Farmers with no electricity, no schools, no roads. The state's answer was bombs. Your answer was — what? Send private armies to protect the landowners who took the land in the first place?"

"We protected communities from —"

"You protected haciendas. You protected cattle ranchers who had taken land by force for three generations and then hired your people when the farmers finally started pushing back." Camilo kept walking, his voice tight. "I know who funded the AUC. I know which names signed the checks. Those men are still in their houses. Still on their land. And the farmers are still gone."

Silence behind him. A long one.

"Mapiripán," Mauricio said. "1997. Your organization. Forty-nine people. Farmers. Five days while the army stood down and watched." He paused. "My uncle was from Mapiripán."

Camilo said nothing.

"Was he one of yours?" Mauricio said. "Or do you not keep those names?"

"I wasn't there in 1997," Camilo said quietly. "I was sixteen years old."

"Your organization was there."

"Yes." A pause. "My organization was there."

They walked in silence. The stars moved imperceptibly.

"Bojayá," Camilo said eventually. "2002. A church. A hundred and nineteen people who had run there because they thought it would protect them. You dropped a gas cylinder through the roof."

"That wasn't —"

"Your front. Your cylinder. Your order." Camilo's voice was flat. "My cousin was in that church."

Mauricio said nothing.

"El Salado," Mauricio said after a long silence. "2000. Sixty people in three days. Your people watched the roads to make sure no one escaped."

Camilo said nothing.

"My mother was from El Salado," Mauricio said. "She got out. But her sister —" He stopped. "Her sister did not."

The grass moved around them. Somewhere an animal crossed the plain at a distance, invisible.

"I'm sorry about your aunt," Camilo said.

"Don't."

"Your uncle and my cousin and your aunt," Camilo said. "That's what this is. That's what it has always been. They give us ideology and we give them our dead."

"Don't say they. You chose this."

"So did you."

"I chose it because your people were burning farms in my department and the state wouldn't move. What was I supposed to —"

"I chose it because the state was burning farms in my department and sending paramilitaries to finish the job. What was I supposed to —"

The sentence stopped. Both of them heard it at the same time — the shape of what they were saying, the identical structure of it, each man finishing the other's sentence from opposite directions.

They walked in silence for a long time after that.

— — —

"You have a family," Mauricio said.

"A daughter. Eight years old."

"What does she think you do?"

"Logistics. Transport."

"Mine knows," Mauricio said. "My son. Twelve. He's proud." A pause. "That's the part I can't fix. I can stop. I can walk away. But I can't make him not proud of what I was." He paused. "Can you fix yours?"

Camilo thought about his daughter's face. The way she said papá when he came through the door.

"No," he said. "I can't fix mine either."

"Then we're the same," Mauricio said. Flatly. The way you state a fact you don't like.

"We're not the same."

"No. But we're not different in the ways that matter."

Camilo had spent eleven years inside an ideology that explained exactly how he was different, how the cause justified the cost, how the accounting would eventually balance. He had believed it for most of those years. He was not sure, walking across the dark Llanos with his hands tied and a paramilitary gun at his spine, how much of it he still believed.

"The farmers are still dead," he said.

"Yes," Mauricio said. "They are."

— — —

They heard it at the same moment.

A whistle — four notes, slow, descending, returning and descending again. From the east. Distant.

Both men stopped.

Neither spoke for a moment.

"What is that," Mauricio said. His voice had changed. Something in it that Camilo had not heard before — not the operational calm, not the compressed anger. Something underneath those things.

"You know what that is," Camilo said.

"I know what it sounds like."

"Your mother told you. About the Llanos."

A pause. "Yes."

"My uncle told me." Camilo's mouth was dry. "The whistle inverts. Close sounds far. Far sounds close."

"That's a story."

"Yes." His voice was not as steady as he wanted it to be. "It's a story." He listened to the four descending notes moving across the dark plain and felt something cold settle in his chest that was not the night air. "We need to move. West. Now."

"You believe it."

"I believe there are sixty-four people in the ground near here and however many of yours somewhere in this corridor, and I believe in the Llanos at night there are things drawn to that. I believe it. Yes." A pause. "Do you?"

Mauricio did not answer right away. Camilo could hear him breathing — could hear the rhythm of it change.

"Yes," Mauricio said. Quietly. Stripped of everything else.

The gun left Camilo's spine.

He turned. Mauricio was looking east, toward the sound, his face doing something complicated. His hand was at his side, the gun loose in it, his posture entirely changed — not the posture of a man holding a prisoner but of a man standing in the open in the dark hearing something that his grandmother had told him about in a specific tone of voice when he was a child.

"The cord," Camilo said.

Mauricio looked at him. Then he put the gun in his waistband and untied the electrical cord from Camilo's wrists without speaking. The blood returned in a rush of pins. Camilo shook his hands.

They turned west together and walked fast, then faster, the whistle behind them, the four notes descending and returning and descending in the dark.

"It's not following," Mauricio said. His breathing was audible now.

"Don't slow down."

"It sounds the same. The same distance."

"That's what I'm telling you. Don't slow down."

They walked for twenty minutes. The whistle came intermittently — always behind, always what seemed like the same distance, or perhaps slightly farther. The volume diminishing.

"It's getting farther," Mauricio said. Something in his voice that wanted very badly to be relief.

"Keep walking."

"I can barely hear it."

"Keep walking."

Camilo focused on the stars. On his daughter's face. On the sensation of his feet and the blood in his hands and the fact of still being alive, still moving —

"I can't hear it anymore," Mauricio said.

Camilo stopped walking.

"What —"

"Don't stop," Camilo said. His voice had changed. "Don't stop walking."

"It's gone. We lost it."

"My uncle said —" He stopped. "My uncle said when you can't hear it anymore —"

He heard the bones.

Not the whistle. Something underneath the whistle, something that had been under it all along but masked by the four notes — a dry rattling, a shifting weight, the specific percussion of many bones in a sack moving together. Close. Directly beside them. On both sides.

Not distant.

Not distant at all.

"Camilo —"

"Don't stop walking. Don't stop, don't look, don't —"

The rattling stopped.

The whistle stopped.

The Llanos were perfectly, completely, absolutely silent.

For a moment — one moment — there was nothing. No wind. No grass sound. No breathing. As if the plain itself had paused.

Then nothing.

— — —

The search parties found the electrical cord three days later, coiled neatly beside a cracked palm. Two sets of boot prints walking west, then stopping. No sign of struggle. No blood. No bodies.

The grass was undisturbed.

The sky above was enormous and indifferent, as it always is above the Llanos, which keep everything and explain nothing.

— — —

El Tiempo, Bogotá — the following Thursday

MASS GRAVE DISCOVERED IN EASTERN META DEPARTMENT

Authorities confirm recovery of remains of approximately sixty-four individuals in remote Llanos site. Evidence consistent with extrajudicial executions carried out by illegal armed group with FARC links, 2009–2016. Investigators say the site was identified following an anonymous tip. Families of the disappeared are urged to contact...

PARAMILITARY BURIAL SITE IDENTIFIED NEAR ARIARI RIVER

Human rights investigators announce location of mass grave containing remains of between seventy and ninety victims, attributed to Autodefensas Gaitanistas operatives active in the corridor between 2014 and 2023. The discovery follows months of investigation into...

The newspaper lay on a plastic table outside a tejo court in Villavicencio. An old man in rubber boots read both headlines, set the paper down, looked east toward the Llanos for a moment — the flat horizon, the enormous sky, the late afternoon light turning everything the color of old bone.

He ordered another beer.

To the east, somewhere past the point where the road ended and the grass began and the plain swallowed everything the plain had decided to keep, the wind moved through the grass.

Just the wind.

Just the grass.

Nothing else.

— — —

The Llanos of eastern Colombia are the site of mass graves attributed to paramilitary groups, FARC guerrillas, and state security forces. Human rights investigators estimate that more than 80,000 people were forcibly disappeared during Colombia's armed conflict. Recovery efforts have identified fewer than 15% of victims.

El Silbón — The Whistler — walks the Llanos carrying a sack of bones. The inversion of his whistle is the detail that has persisted across every version of the legend for centuries: close sounds far, far sounds close. By the time you understand the distance correctly, it no longer matters.

The bones in the sack, the old stories say, are not always strangers' bones. Sometimes they belong to El Silbón himself — everything he has carried so long it has become part of him. Folklorists have noted that no version of the story explains how to tell the difference.

— — —

06

La Madremonte

Root System

Caquetá, Colombian Amazon · April · 2026

Root System

The first thing Brad Koller did when he landed in Florencia was check his phone.

No signal. He had been warned about this — the company's Colombia coordinator had told him, twice, that connectivity in Caquetá was unreliable and that the field team used satellite communicators. He knew this. He had packed a satellite communicator. He checked his phone anyway, the way Americans check their phones, which is to say reflexively, the way you check a wound.

He was forty-seven, VP of International Operations for Crestfield Natural Resources Inc., based in Birmingham, Alabama. Crestfield was a mid-sized extractive company — coal primarily, some metals, a growing portfolio of what the investor materials called "critical mineral exploration" in regions where, as Brad liked to say in presentations, the regulatory environment presented opportunities. He had managed projects in six countries. He had never managed a project that had eaten three people.

Eaten was not the word in the incident reports. The incident reports said unaccounted for and temporarily separated from the team and, in the case of the last one, location currently unknown pending search operations. Brad had written the phrase location currently unknown himself, in an email to Crestfield's legal team, and had felt even as he typed it that it was the most dishonest thing he had ever put in a document, which was a high bar for a man who wrote investor materials for a living.

He had come to Caquetá because three members of his survey team were gone. He had told himself he was coming because it was the right thing to do. He had also told himself he was coming because if this project failed — if the coltan concession was abandoned without completing the preliminary survey — he would need to explain to the board why fourteen million dollars of exploration budget had produced nothing, and location currently unknown was not an explanation the board would accept.

Both of these things were true. He had learned, at forty-seven, that most things were true in at least two directions at once.

— — —

The concession covered eleven thousand hectares in the Caquetá department, legally registered, properly permitted, signed by the relevant officials in Bogotá — which was, as Brad had occasion to reflect on the four-hour drive from Florencia into the jungle, a very long way from eleven thousand hectares of old-growth Amazon. The permits had taken eight months and two consulting firms and a government relations budget that Brad had categorized under administrative costs in the investor materials.

What the permits had not addressed — what Brad's government relations consultants had advised him, twice, in writing, was a manageable complication — was ILO Convention 169. The International Labour Organization's convention on indigenous peoples' rights required free, prior, and informed consent before any extractive activity on ancestral lands. The Uitoto community whose territory overlapped with approximately sixty percent of the concession block had filed a formal objection eighteen months ago.

The objection was before a tribunal in Bogotá. Brad's lawyers called it pending resolution. The Uitoto's lawyer — a woman named Lucía Andoke, whose emails Brad had been forwarding unread to legal for eleven months — called it a fundamental violation of international law.

Brad's legal team had advised him that the tribunal process could take two to four years and that survey operations could proceed in the interim. This was technically accurate and had been enough for Brad, who was a practical man.

He was thinking about this on the drive — specifically, he was thinking about the email Lucía Andoke had sent him three days before his flight, which he had almost forwarded unread to legal but had instead, for reasons he couldn't articulate, actually opened. It was very short. It said: Mr. Koller. I am asking you one more time to suspend operations. The forest has been asked to protect itself. What is happening to your team is the beginning. Please do not come.

He had forwarded it to legal after reading it.

He had come anyway.

— — —

The remaining team was two men — Guerrero, the Colombian project manager who had been running the ground operations, and a young geologist named Salinas who had arrived as a replacement two weeks ago and who had the specific alertness of someone who has been told things that he is still deciding whether to believe.

They met Brad at the equipment depot, a clearing hacked out of the jungle edge where the trucks parked and the generators ran and the satellite uplink worked intermittently. Guerrero shook his hand with the grip of a man who has been waiting for someone with authority to arrive and is now reconsidering whether authority will be useful here.

"Tell me about the disappearances," Brad said.

Guerrero told him. Ríos first — the equipment arranged at the base of the fig tree, the hard hat, the GPS unit. Then Prada, the geologist found at dusk at the survey perimeter, unable to account for six hours, repeating quietly that the forest was watching. Then Castillo, found in a clearing that the satellite imagery said didn't exist, calm in a way that was not calm, saying: she was made of the forest, not like a metaphor, actually.

Brad listened. He took notes on his tablet. He asked the kinds of questions project managers ask: Were proper protocols followed? Were the men experienced? Were there any signs of foul play from external actors — illegal miners, coca growers, anyone with a territorial interest in the concession block?

"No," Guerrero said.

"Then what do you think happened?"

Guerrero looked at him for a long moment. "I think the forest happened," he said.

Brad wrote this down. He labeled it: Environmental factors, investigation pending.

— — —

He heard it the first night.

He was alone in the equipment depot's sleeping unit — a converted shipping container, air-conditioned to a temperature that was exactly right for an office in Birmingham and exactly wrong for the jungle, which made itself known anyway in the sounds that came through the metal walls. The insects were a constant — not background noise but foreground noise, layered and specific, and Brad had been told he would get used to it and had not gotten used to it.

Underneath the insects, something else.

A weight moving through vegetation at a distance — heavy, unhurried, with the specific rhythm of something that does not need to be quiet because it is not afraid of anything in this forest. It circled the clearing once. He was certain of this — he tracked it by sound, east to south to west to north and back east again, a full circuit of the camp's perimeter in the dark.

Then it stopped.

He could not tell where. The insects continued. Nothing else moved.

Brad lay on his cot and told himself: jaguar. Large male. Curious about the camp. This happened. He had read about this.

He fell asleep with the light on.

In the morning, before the others were up, he walked the path between the sleeping unit and the equipment depot — thirty meters, packed dirt, clearly defined. Or it had been clearly defined. He stopped at the edge of the sleeping unit's door and looked at what the night had done to it.

The path was covered. Not overgrown — covered, the way you cover something deliberately. Broad leaves and creeping vines laid across the packed dirt in a density that would have taken weeks to grow. It ran the full thirty meters. It ended cleanly at the depot door, as if the vegetation had known where to stop.

He stood there for a long time.

He went back inside. He did not mention it when the others woke. He told Guerrero to have the path cleared and gave no reason and Guerrero gave him a look that meant he already knew the reason.

He did not put it in his report.

— — —

She appeared to him on the second afternoon.

He had gone alone to the survey grid's northern boundary to check a GPS marker that Salinas had flagged as misaligned — a twenty-minute walk from camp, a routine task, the kind of thing he did to feel useful in a situation where his usefulness was unclear. He had his tablet and his satellite communicator and he had told Guerrero where he was going.

He found the marker. He crouched to check it. He stood.

She was at the treeline. Twelve meters away. Possibly less.

He had not heard her approach. She had simply become present — the way the jungle itself was present, the way the green was present, because she was both of those things. Tall in the way the surrounding trees were tall, covered in vegetation not as clothing but as substance, as material, the green not on her but of her. Her face — he could see the face at twelve meters, he could not look away from it — was the face of something that had been patient for a very long time and had now run out of patience.

She was looking at him with the full attention of a thing that has been watching something grow worse and worse and has decided that it has grown worse enough.

Brad took one step back.

She took one step forward.

The step was wrong. Not wrong in the way a person's step is wrong — wrong in the way a tree moves in a storm, a displacement of more weight than should be moving, a suggestion of roots that extended further than anything visible. The ground beneath his feet shifted slightly when she moved, as if they were connected through the soil.

He ran.

He ran the full twenty minutes back to camp without stopping, without looking back, crashing through the undergrowth where the path was not clear, his tablet lost somewhere behind him, his satellite communicator bouncing against his chest. He ran until he could see the depot's metal roof and the generator cable and the ordinary human geometry of the camp, and he stopped at the edge of the clearing with his hands on his knees and his lungs making sounds he did not recognize.

He stood there for two minutes.

Then he walked into the depot and poured water on his face and went to find Guerrero.

"I dropped my tablet at the northern marker," he said. His voice was almost steady. "Can someone retrieve it?"

Guerrero looked at him. "Did you see it," he said.

Brad poured more water. "Get someone to retrieve the tablet."

Guerrero nodded slowly. "I'll go myself," he said. "No one else goes to the northern boundary alone."

"Thank you," Brad said.

He went to his container and sat on the cot and looked at his hands, which were shaking, and waited for them to stop. They took longer than he expected.

— — —

She came inside on the second night.

He had locked the container door. He had checked the lock three times. He lay on the cot in the dark — he had turned the light off because he did not want to see anything, which was a logic he understood was not sound and which he applied anyway — and he listened to the jungle and the insects and the generator's distant hum.

The insects stopped at 1 a.m.

He knew the time because he had been watching the clock on his phone, which was the only light in the container and which he held against his chest so the screen would not be visible if anything was looking through the air vents.

He was aware that this was not a rational precaution. He took it anyway.

The smell came first — the deep forest-floor cold, wet earth and root systems and the specific darkness of places where no sunlight had reached in decades. Inside the sealed, locked, air-conditioned container. Not faint this time. Not a trace. Full, the way the jungle smelled when you were inside it, the smell of being surrounded.

Then the temperature dropped. Not the air conditioning adjusting — the air conditioning had stopped, as it had the night before, as if a decision had been made about it. The temperature dropped the way it drops in the deep forest at elevation, sudden and complete.

He did not move.

The door — the locked door, the door he had checked three times — opened.

Not violently. Not forced. It opened the way a door opens when someone with a key uses it, smoothly, with the ordinary sound of the latch, and the jungle came in. Not metaphorically — the smell increased to the point where he was breathing forest air, root air, the air of a place that predated every human decision that had brought him to this container. The insects outside were audible now through the open door. They did not come in.

Nothing came in that he could see.

But the container changed. He felt it before he understood it — the dimensions altered, or his sense of them altered, the walls receding slightly in his peripheral vision, the ceiling rising, the space becoming less container and more something else, something that had the geometry of a place where roots went and light did not. The air pressed against him with the specific density of very old air, air that had been cycling through the same closed system for longer than he had been alive.

He could hear breathing. Not his own.

Slow. Patient. The breathing of something that was measuring him, that had been measuring everything about him since he arrived, that had already completed its assessment and was now simply present in the way a verdict is present before it is spoken.

"I'm leaving," he said. His voice came out at a volume he could barely hear. "I'm leaving tomorrow. I'm suspending the project. I'm — please. I'm leaving."

The breathing continued for a moment.

Then the door closed. On its own, with the same smooth ordinary sound of the latch.

The air conditioning came back on.

The smell faded by degrees, slowly, the way a very deep thing fades — not all at once but in layers, the top layer first, and then the next, and underneath each layer another layer, until finally it was just the container again, just the recycled manufactured air, just the clock on his phone reading 1:47 a.m.

The insects started again.

Brad sat up on the cot. He sat there until the sky through the air vents began to lighten. He did not lie back down. He did not close his eyes. He sat with his knees pulled to his chest in the position of a person making themselves as small as possible, and he waited for morning with the specific patience of a man who has understood something and cannot misunderstand it.

At 5:30 a.m. he began to pack.

— — —

In the morning he called Crestfield's legal team in Birmingham. He asked them, specifically, to walk him through the ILO 169 exposure. Not the tribunal process — the exposure. What were the actual risks if the tribunal ruled against the concession while survey operations had continued.

The lawyer was a man named Perkins who had a voice like a document — flat, organized, without inflection.

Perkins talked for twenty minutes. He talked about reputational risk and investor sensitivity and the current ESG environment and the increasing scrutiny on indigenous land rights in supply chains. He talked about the Uitoto community's lawyer and her track record and the fact that she had, in the last eleven months, gotten three international human rights organizations interested in the case and one journalist from a major outlet asking questions.

"What's your read on the tribunal?" Brad said.

A pause. "Honestly? I think they rule against us. I've thought that for about six months."

"Why didn't you tell me?"

Another pause. "You didn't ask for my honest read. You asked if operations could continue."

Brad looked out the window of the depot office at the jungle, which stood at the edge of the cleared area in the morning light and was entirely itself — green and indifferent and old, old in a way that made his fourteen-million-dollar concession feel like a small, recent, and temporary idea.

"If we suspend voluntarily," Brad said. "Before the ruling. Is that better for us?"

"Significantly."

"Enough to matter to the board?"

"Coupled with the operational issues —" Perkins paused again. "You've had three people disappear, Brad. That's a liability exposure independent of the indigenous rights question."

Brad thought about the door. The smell. The thing that had moved along the outside of the container at 2 a.m. the way you move when you are not afraid of anything in this forest.

"What's the coltan situation in Mozambique?" he said.

"I'd have to check."

"Check," Brad said. "And get me the suspension paperwork."

— — —

He was packed in forty minutes.

Guerrero, when Brad told him, looked at him with the expression of a man who had been waiting for this conversation and had not been sure it would come. He shook Brad's hand — a different grip this time.

"The people who disappeared," Brad said. "Do you think they'll come back?"

Guerrero looked at the jungle. "I think they're where they're supposed to be now," he said, which was not an answer Brad could put in a report but which was, he had come to believe, probably the truest thing anyone had said on this project.

He drove to Florencia. He caught the afternoon flight to Bogotá. He caught the connection to Miami and the connection to Birmingham. On the plane, somewhere over the Caribbean, he opened his laptop and began drafting the Mozambique proposal.

The Cabo Delgado block had been in Crestfield's pipeline for two years — a graphite deposit, exceptional concentration, favorable government relationships, the kind of situation his investor materials would describe as a compelling first-mover opportunity in an underexplored jurisdiction. He had visited once, briefly, and found the terrain manageable and the local officials cooperative. The permits were already moving.

He wrote for three hours. By the time they crossed Florida he had the budget reallocation framed as a strategic pivot — disciplined capital deployment in response to evolving regulatory conditions — which was the kind of sentence that made boards feel that problems were actually decisions. He was good at this. He had always been good at this.

He also wrote an email to Lucía Andoke. Three sentences. Ms. Andoke. Crestfield is suspending operations in the Caquetá block pending proper consultation with your community. I should have done this earlier. I'm sorry.

He sent it on landing and did not think about it again.

— — —

The Mozambique kick-off call was three weeks later.

The Cabo Delgado block overlapped, it turned out, with territory used by the Makua-Metto people, who had farmed and fished it for generations and who had not been consulted about the graphite concession. The company's Maputo-based coordinator mentioned this on the call — briefly, as a line item under community relations, the way you mention a weather forecast when you are already committed to the trip.

"Is there a legal framework issue?" Brad asked.

"Mozambique hasn't ratified ILO 169," the coordinator said.

"Good," Brad said, and moved to the next item.

The field team was scheduled to begin preliminary surveys in six weeks. The coordinator sent Brad the survey grid two days later. In the notes section, almost as an afterthought, he had written: Local communities report unusual activity at the northern boundary of the concession block. Unclear nature. Flagging for awareness.

Brad read it. He forwarded it to the operations team with a note: Keep me posted.

He closed the email.

He opened the Mozambique budget model and looked at the graphite concentration numbers, which were very good, which were in fact exceptional, and he felt them doing what numbers always did for him — organizing the available information into a frame, a structure, something that held.

He had always found numbers settling.

Outside his Birmingham office the afternoon light came through the blinds in flat columns and the air conditioning ran clean and controlled and the city went on in every direction, orderly and certain, nothing in it older than what men had built.

He kept working.

— — —

Colombia's Amazon basin has lost more than 200,000 hectares of forest annually since 2016, driven by extractive industries, cattle ranching, and illegal agriculture. Indigenous communities hold legal title to approximately 30% of the Colombian Amazon but face continuous encroachment.

ILO Convention 169, ratified by Colombia in 1991, requires free, prior, and informed consent from indigenous communities before extractive or development activities on their ancestral lands. As of 2026, Mozambique has not ratified the convention.

La Madremonte is a figure from Colombian Andean and Amazon folklore — a guardian of the forest, clothed in vegetation, who disorients and drives away those who threaten the wild places under her protection. She does not distinguish between the powerful and the powerless. She distinguishes only between those who belong and those who do not.

She is not the only one.

— — —

07

El Familiar

The Terms of the Agreement

Tucumán Province, Argentina · June to November · 2026

The Terms of the Agreement

The sugar harvest in Tucumán ran from June to November, and every year without fail, men died.

The provincial labor authority's records showed an average of three to five fatalities per season across the department's seventeen major mills — machinery accidents, heat exhaustion, the occasional fall. The numbers were consistent enough to be unremarkable, which was itself a kind of remark that no one in the authority had made in the eleven years that Valentina Greco had been doing this work.

Valentina was a labor rights investigator — freelance, underpaid, operating out of a two-room office in San Miguel de Tucumán. She had no authority to compel testimony, no power to shut anything down, no institutional backing beyond a small NGO in Buenos Aires that covered roughly two-thirds of her expenses. What she had was eleven years of records, a red pen, and the specific stubbornness of a person who has decided that the most important thing she can do with her life is make certain things visible that would prefer to remain invisible.

The mill was called Ingenio San Custodio. It had operated continuously since 1887. It had always survived. It had always produced. Its sugar was in every supermarket in the northwest, in brands that carried no trace of San Custodio's name.

Three deaths per season, every season, for eleven years of her records. Going back forty years in the provincial archive, the number was the same. Three per season — not two in a bad year, not five in a worse one. Three. With a consistency that was not the consistency of accident but of arrangement.

She had a source inside the mill. She had gone to meet him.

— — —

I. The Bar in Monteros

Domingo Ríos Castellano was sixty-three, broad across the shoulders, with the hands of someone who had been cutting sugarcane since he was fourteen. He had worked at San Custodio for thirty-one years. He told her this before anything else, as if the number were relevant to everything that followed — which, she came to understand, it was.

He had chosen a bar in Monteros, twenty minutes from the mill, where no one from San Custodio drank. He arrived before her and had already ordered, and he sat with his beer the way men sit when they have made a decision and are now living inside it.

"I retire in March," he said. "End of the next harvest. Thirty-two years and then I'm done." He turned his glass on the table. "I've been thinking about what I carry out with me when I go. What I leave behind." He looked up. "I don't want to carry this out. So I need to give it to someone."

"I'm listening," Valentina said.

"The deaths," he said. "They're always the same men. Not the same men — the same kind." He turned his glass again. "New ones. Men who just arrived. Men nobody knows yet."

Valentina wrote this down.

"They come from the north. Bolivia, mostly. Some from Paraguay. They come at the start of the harvest because the work is there and the pay is better than home and because nobody tells them what the mill is." He paused. "Nobody tells them what the mill requires."

"What does it require?" she said.

Domingo was quiet for a long moment. Outside, a truck passed and the windows rattled and settled.

"My grandfather worked at San Custodio," he said. "His grandfather before him. There is a story in my family." He looked at his glass. "There is a story in every family that has worked at that mill for long enough. You stop saying it out loud after a while. You stop saying it because you know, and the knowing is enough, and saying it makes it something you have to decide about." He paused. "I've been deciding for thirty-one years. I retire in March."

"Tell me the story," Valentina said.

"The first owner — Custodio Ferreira, 1887 — made an agreement," Domingo said. "With something that lives in the cane. Something old. The agreement was: the mill prospers, the harvest never fails, no drought touches these fields." He paused. "And in return — three per season. Three who are new. Three who have no one to ask questions."

The bar was quiet. The television in the corner showed football with the sound off.

"You think this is superstition," he said.

"I think three deaths per season for forty years is a pattern that requires explanation," Valentina said. "Tell me about this season."

"Two so far," he said. "One in June. One in August. Both new. Both from the north." He wrapped both hands around his glass. "The season closes in November."

"Meaning there's one more to come."

"There's always one more to come," he said.

She looked at him across the table — this large, careful man with the cane-cutter's hands and thirty-one years of knowing — and thought about the weight of carrying a thing for that long without saying it.

"Why me?" she said. "Why now?"

He was quiet for a moment. Then: "Because I'm going to retire in March. And then I'm going to spend the rest of my life knowing what I know." He looked at his hands. "I'd rather spend it knowing I gave it to someone who could do something with it." He looked up. "Can you do something with it?"

"I don't know," she said. "But I'll try."

He nodded. He finished his beer. He told her the names of the two dead men, the dates, the locations. He told her which supervisor had processed the paperwork on each. He told her three other names — men who had been at the mill long enough to know, who would never speak to her but whose silence she could at least document.

He left first. She sat with her notes and thought about what it cost to carry something for thirty-one years and what it cost to put it down.

— — —

II. The Research

The Registro Civil of the municipality of Monteros occupied the ground floor of a building that had been doing this work since 1923, which you could tell from the quality of its floors and the specific smell of its air — old paper, old ink, the particular stillness of a room where things are stored that people sometimes desperately need and more often prefer to forget. The clerk who processed Valentina's information request was a woman in her sixties who handled the folders the way you handle things you have handled ten thousand times, without looking at them, with a competence so complete it had become invisible.

The first death had been in June. A Bolivian man named Rufino Quispe, twenty-nine, caught in a cane transport mechanism that every worker at the mill knew to avoid and every new worker was supposed to be warned about on their first day. The accident report noted that Quispe had not received the standard safety orientation. The mill's HR records — she had obtained these separately, through a formal request that had taken three weeks and two follow-up letters — showed that he had signed the orientation form. The signature did not match any other document Quispe had signed.

The second death was in August. A Paraguayan man named Lorenzo Báez, thirty-four. Heat exhaustion, found in a section of the mill where workers were not supposed to be during peak hours. No explanation for how he had gotten there, or why the safety door to that section had been unlocked, or why the cooling system had been offline for six hours without anyone logging the fault.

She was reading the Báez report when she became aware of the dog.

It was at the far end of the records room, near the shelving that held the oldest registers — the ones from the late nineteenth century, labeled in a hand that had been precise once and was now just legible. A black dog, large, sitting in the narrow space between two shelving units with the specific stillness of something that has been there for some time and intends to remain. Not chained, not collared. Not doing anything. Just present in the way a thing is present when it belongs somewhere.

Valentina looked at it. It did not look at her.

She looked at the clerk, who was at her desk filling in a ledger with the same invisible competence. The clerk did not look at the dog.

Valentina looked back at the Báez report. She read the next paragraph — the signed cooling system log, the maintenance supervisor whose name she would later be unable to find in any payroll record — and when she looked up again the dog was gone. The space between the shelving units was empty. She had not heard it move.

She sat for a moment.

Then she turned back to the documents, because that was what she did when things did not fit into any category she had — she returned to the documents, which at least had the decency to be legible.

The shape of the absent information was familiar. She had seen it before in other mills, other industries — the unsigned form that was signed, the door that shouldn't have been open. The infrastructure of an accident prepared in advance and labeled after the fact. She had filed fourteen complaints with the labor authority in eleven years. Eleven had been closed without action. Two were pending. One had resulted in a fine the mill had paid in forty-eight hours — faster than any fine she had ever seen paid, which told her something about how much the fine had cost relative to everything else.

She had also, pulling the property and corporate registers from the same archive, found something she had not been looking for.

The mill's ownership was a shelf company in Uruguay, owned by a Cayman Islands holding, connected through remarkable complexity to a family trust whose name was Ferreira. The same family. One hundred and thirty-seven years of continuous ownership behind one hundred and thirty-seven years of corporate structure, each generation making it less visible and more defensible.

She called the NGO contact from the car park outside, because the records room had made her want to be in open air.

"The trust," she said. "Is there documentation of the terms?"

"There's an original trust document from 1887, notarized in Tucumán." A pause. "It's unusual." He read the key clause to her over the phone, translating from the legal Spanish: The operation of the estate and its associated commercial activities shall be maintained in perpetuity in accordance with the foundational agreement of June 3, 1887, the terms of which are separately recorded and binding on all successors.

"What's the separately recorded document?"

"It doesn't appear to exist in any public registry. But the trust references it as if it's the primary instrument — everything else is subordinate to it."

"The board," she said. "The current directors. Do they know?"

"They signed a document at appointment acknowledging fiduciary obligation to all governing instruments." A pause. "Including the agreement of June 3, 1887."

She stood in the car park for a while after the call ended. The afternoon was warm and ordinary. Someone's radio played cumbia from an open window above the pharmacy across the road.

The pact had been incorporated into governance. The board had signed it. Every successor had signed it. One hundred and thirty-seven years of executives acknowledging, in writing, the terms of an arrangement with something that lived in the cane.

Something that also, apparently, sat in records offices.

She got in the car. She added it to the file. She labeled the section: Knowing participation.

— — —

III. The Descendant

The original Ferreira estate was twelve kilometers from the mill, at the end of a dirt road that the map showed and the road itself seemed uncertain about. The house had been built in 1887 — the same year as the trust, the same year as the agreement — and had not been substantially modified since. The veranda columns were darkened by decades of wet season. The bougainvillea was so old it had become structural, its roots in the walls.

Isabela Ferreira Montes had agreed to meet her here rather than in the city. Family matters on family property, she had said. Valentina had interpreted this as proprietary. Standing in front of the house in the flat late afternoon light, she interpreted it differently.

The estate felt inhabited in a way that had nothing to do with the woman waiting on the veranda.

Not haunted — that was the wrong word, implying something residual, something leftover. This felt active. The cane fields began fifty meters from the house and ran to the horizon in every direction, and they were moving in a wind Valentina could not feel on her own skin. The stalks bent and straightened in patterns that were almost rhythmic, almost deliberate, the way a large animal moves through tall grass when it does not want to be seen but does not particularly care whether it is heard.

She heard it in the cane as she walked to the veranda. A low, slow movement. Heavy. Unhurried.

Isabela Ferreira Montes was fifty-six, composed, dressed for a business meeting in a house that had not been a business for a long time. She offered nothing — no coffee, no water — and gestured to a chair across from hers on the veranda as if conducting an interview she had prepared for.

"The mill has been in my family for five generations," she said. "We're proud of what it represents."

"Three workers die there every season," Valentina said. "Every season for at least forty years."

"The sugar industry carries inherent risks."

"The deaths are always new workers. Men who've just arrived from Bolivia or Paraguay. Men with no established relationships in the region."

Isabela Ferreira Montes looked past her, toward the cane fields. "I don't think that pattern exists in the way you're suggesting."

Valentina heard the movement in the cane again — closer now, or seeming closer. She turned her head slightly. The stalks at the nearest edge of the field were bending without wind, in a slow, specific way, something pushing through them from inside.

"The foundational agreement," Valentina said. "June 3, 1887. Are you aware of it?"

The movement in the cane stopped.

The silence that followed was not the silence of wind dying or an animal going still. It was a listening silence — the quality of air in a room when something in it has turned its attention toward a sound.

Isabela Ferreira Montes did not look at the cane. She kept her eyes on Valentina with a steadiness that was, Valentina understood now, not composure but practice — the practiced steadiness of a person who has learned not to look.

"I'm not sure what document you're referring to," she said.

"Your family's trust from 1887 references it as the primary governing instrument," Valentina said. Her voice was even. She was concentrating on keeping it even. "Every director of the operating company signs documents at appointment acknowledging fiduciary obligation to its terms. You signed one yourself in 2009."

Something came out of the cane.

A dog — black, the size of something larger than a dog should be, moving with the specific unhurried quality of a thing that does not need to hurry because it has already arrived wherever it intended to be. It came through the cane's edge and crossed the open ground between the field and the house without looking at anything. Without looking at Valentina.

It stopped at the base of the veranda steps.

It sat.

Isabela Ferreira Montes did not look at it. She did not react in any way that indicated she had seen it. She kept her eyes on Valentina and her hands folded in her lap and her expression exactly as it had been.

Valentina looked at the dog. The dog did not look at her.

It was looking at Isabela Ferreira Montes. With the patient, fixed attention of something that has been part of an arrangement for a long time and has come to confirm that the arrangement continues.

"My family has honored its commitments for five generations," Isabela Ferreira Montes said. "We intend to continue doing so."

It was not a denial. It was not, Valentina understood now, addressed to her.

She stood. Her legs were steady. She was grateful for this.

"Thank you for your time," she said.

She walked off the veranda. She walked past the dog, which did not move, did not turn, continued to look at

Isabela Ferreira Montes with the same patient attention. She walked to her car. She did not look back at the house, or the cane, or the thing at the base of the steps.

She drove the twelve kilometers of dirt road with both hands on the wheel and the windows up. She drove until the dirt became asphalt and the cane fields gave way to streetlights and traffic and the ordinary sounds of people living their ordinary lives.

She pulled over. She sat for a moment. Then she took out her phone and added a single line to her notes, the section marked not for distribution:

It is real. It is there. It knows what it is owed.

She saved the file.

She drove back to her office.

— — —

IV. The Third Death

Valentina heard about it from Celia, who had seen it in the provincial newspaper's brief labor incident column — four lines, below an advertisement for a hardware store. A worker at Ingenio San Custodio. Fatal fall in the cane fields during night operations. Name withheld pending notification of family.

She knew before she called the mill's HR office. She knew in the way you know things when you have been paying attention long enough — the shape of it, the timing of it, the specific location of it in the season's calendar.

His name was Domingo Ríos Castellano. Sixty-three years old. Thirty-one years at the mill.

Not a new worker. Not a man from Bolivia or Paraguay with no one to ask questions. A man everyone at San Custodio knew, who had been there longer than most, who had four months left before retirement.

Who had, six weeks earlier, sat in a bar in Monteros and given his thirty-one years of silence to a labor rights investigator he had decided to trust.

Valentina sat at her desk for a long time.

She thought about the pattern — always new workers, always unknown, always men with no one to ask questions. She thought about how Domingo had broken it. Whether the pact adjusted for anyone who became a liability, or whether there was something older at work — something that had noted what Domingo had done and recategorized him accordingly.

She thought about the bar in Monteros. His hands on the glass. I don't want to carry this out. So I need to give it to someone.

She had taken it. She had taken what he gave her and done what she did with everything — filed it, documented it, built a case around it. And Domingo had gone back to the mill for four more months, because he needed the pension, because thirty-one years entitled him to it, because you don't walk away from thirty-one years four months before the end.

She filed the complaint on a Monday. Not just labor authority and ministry — the criminal prosecutor's office, with a cover letter laying out the pattern, the trust document, Isabela Ferreira Montes's non-denial, and the fact that the third death this season was a long-term employee who had recently provided testimony to a labor rights investigator. She used the word retaliation. She used the word homicide.

She did not expect it to go anywhere. She filed it anyway.

She thought about the separately recorded foundational agreement — the one that existed in no registry, that governed everything and could be found nowhere. She thought about what it would take to find it. How many years.

She thought about Domingo, who had given her thirty-one years of knowing and had four months left and had gone back anyway.

Her phone buzzed.

A message from Celia: New referral. Textile mill in Santiago del Estero. Four deaths this season, all subcontracted workers from Salta, all documentation missing. Family of one victim has been trying to find someone for six months. They have nowhere else to go.

Valentina read it.

She looked at the San Custodio file. At the question of the foundational agreement that existed nowhere and explained everything. At Domingo's number still in her phone, which she would never call again.

She saved the file.

She opened a new one.

Santiago del Estero — textile, 4 deaths, subcontracted workers.

She began to type.

— — —

The Tucumán sugar industry employs approximately 60,000 seasonal workers per harvest, the majority migrating from Bolivia, Paraguay, and northern Argentina. Labor rights organizations report persistent violations including wage theft, unsafe conditions, and inadequate safety training for seasonal workers. Fatality rates in the industry consistently exceed national averages.

El Familiar is a figure from Argentine, Bolivian, and northwestern folklore — a demon, often appearing as a black dog or serpent, that inhabits sugar mills and other large estates. The owner enters into a pact: prosperity and protection in exchange for a periodic human sacrifice, typically a worker who is new and unknown. The legend has been documented in Tucumán continuously since the late nineteenth century. Labor historians have noted that it emerged simultaneously with the expansion of the industrial sugar industry and the importation of migrant labor.

The connection between the legend and the labor conditions it describes has not been lost on those who study it.

— — —

08

El Pishtaco

What the Body Owes

Chinchero, Cusco, Peru · March to January · 2025–2026

What the Body Owes

The clinic opened on a Saturday in March, and the village celebrated.

This was not an exaggeration. Chinchero had not had a permanent health facility since the government post closed three years earlier — closed not dramatically, not with an announcement, but in the slow bureaucratic way of things that stop being funded: the doctor reassigned, the nurse's contract not renewed, the building left with a padlock and a sign saying Temporalmente Cerrado that had yellowed in the sun until the word temporary became a kind of joke the village told itself. Forty minutes by road to the nearest clinic in Urubamba, on roads that became rivers in the wet season. People had managed, the way people manage when managing is the only option available.

So when the Andean Community Health Initiative arrived — with its refurbished building, its solar panels, its generator, its free consultations and free vaccinations and free prenatal care — the village received it the way you receive something you have been needing for a long time and had stopped expecting.

No one could say precisely who had sent them.

The mayor had received a letter, months earlier, from an organization with a long name that translated roughly as the Andean Community Health Initiative. The letterhead showed a small logo — a stylized mountain, a caduceus — but no address beyond a postal box in Lima. When he had called the number at the bottom, a pleasant woman had confirmed the program's details and offered to answer questions, and he had asked the questions that mattered — was it free, yes; was it permanent, we intend for it to be; was it legitimate, we have all necessary registrations — and he had been satisfied, because the answers were the ones he needed.

There were doctors. That much was clear. Two who spoke Spanish with the accent of Lima, and a rotating team of others — four, sometimes five — who spoke Spanish with no accent that anyone in Chinchero could place. Not European, exactly. Not American. Somewhere the village had no reference for. They were tall, most of them. They had the careful, pleasant manner of people who have spent time learning to put communities at ease. They wore their white coats the way visitors wore traditional dress at festivals — correctly, but as a gesture.

There was a ceremony. The mayor spoke. The lead doctor — a tall man, pale in the way that people from elsewhere were pale, who introduced himself simply as Dr. Vargas, though this name fit him the way borrowed clothes fit — spoke through one of the Lima doctors. Children from the school performed. Sisa Mamani, the community health nurse who had been managing without a facility for two years, stood in the back and felt something she recognized as hope and filed under professional development, because she had learned not to invest hope in things that had not yet proven themselves.

She watched Dr. Vargas shake hands. She watched his eyes move across the crowd with a quality she could not quite name — attentive, satisfied, the look of a man arriving at something he has planned for.

She filed this under first impressions, subject to revision.

She went home and did not think about it again for four months.

— — —

I. The Weakening

It was Doña Celestina who she noticed first.

Doña Celestina was seventy-two, strong in the way that women who have worked at altitude their whole lives are strong — not muscular, not robust, but dense, compacted, built for endurance rather than speed. She had climbed to the high pastures every week for sixty years. She had buried two husbands and a son. She had the constitution of someone the mountains had decided to keep.

In July, four months after the clinic opened, she came to Sisa's house and sat in the chair by the door and said: I don't know what's wrong with me.

Sisa asked questions. No fever. No pain. No shortness of breath, no swelling, no change in appetite. Just — less. She used the Quechua word that meant something between lighter and further away. As if some portion of her had been moved to a greater distance from herself.

When did it start? Sisa asked.

Doña Celestina thought about it. After the blood tests, she said. Then, as if correcting herself: A little while after.

Sisa did the blood tests herself — a full panel, sent to the lab in Cusco. Everything normal. Blood pressure normal. Hemoglobin normal. Thyroid normal. She referred Doña Celestina to the clinic for a more comprehensive workup. Dr. Vargas's team ran their own tests and found nothing. They prescribed a multivitamin and suggested more rest.

Doña Celestina was not a woman who rested.

By September there were others. Not many at first — seven, then twelve, then eighteen people who came to Sisa with some version of the same description. Not sick. Not diagnosable. Just reduced. The word kept occurring to her — reduced — though she could not have explained in clinical terms what it meant. They were present in their bodies in the way they had always been, and yet something was different, something that no instrument she had access to could measure, that existed in the space between what a test showed and what a person felt.

She was not the only one who noticed. The village noticed in its own way — the way villages notice things that cannot be said directly, in the register of the almost-spoken, the significant pause, the conversations that stopped when she entered a room and resumed at a different level after she left. She heard the word once, from an old man who said it under his breath as Dr. Vargas crossed the square — said it in Quechua, the old word, the one she had not heard since childhood.

Pishtaco.

She wrote this in her own records, the parallel system she had always kept — not the Initiative's records, her own, in a notebook that lived in her kitchen drawer. She wrote it and looked at it for a long time and thought about her grandmother.

— — —

II. The Investigation

Her grandmother had told her about el Pishtaco when Sisa was twelve, in the kitchen of this same house, while preparing the evening meal.

A man who comes from outside, she had said. Always from outside. He finds you when you are not paying attention — at a health post, at a market, somewhere you have gone because you needed something. He takes from the body what the body makes that has value to him. Not blood — something deeper than blood. The life the blood carries. He takes it carefully, in small amounts, so that you don't notice at first. You feel tired. You feel far from yourself. You feel as if you are still there but less of you is there than before.

How do you stop him? Sisa had asked.

Her grandmother had given her the look she reserved for questions that missed the point. You learn to see him before he sees you.

Sisa had been a twelve-year-old in the process of becoming a scientist. She had filed the story under folklore, significant cultural value, not clinically relevant. She was revising this classification now.

She began asking questions she had not asked at the opening — questions she had not asked because the clinic's arrival had felt like a gift, and gifts make you not ask questions.

No one in the village knew who funded the Initiative. The mayor's letter had come from a Lima postal box that, when Sisa wrote to it, returned no reply. The Initiative's registration listed a parent organization with a name she did not recognize and an address in a country she could not easily verify from Chinchero.

The foreign doctors were more interesting.

She had assumed, initially, that they were European — the coloring, the height, the particular blank pleasantness of certain kinds of outsiders who arrive in communities like this with a project. But one of the nurses said she had heard them talking to each other in a language she could not identify. Not Spanish. Not English. Not anything she had studied. A language that seemed assembled from several others, almost familiar and wasn't.

She asked one of them directly, on a day when she found him alone in the clinic's courtyard. Where are you from?

He had pale eyes that were difficult to read. We're here under a collaborative research arrangement. A multi-country initiative.

Which countries?

He smiled. Many, he said. And looked back at his documents.

What she could establish was this: the Initiative was collecting blood samples, tissue samples, and detailed family health histories going three generations back. The consent forms were in Spanish. The community's understanding of what they were consenting to — she established this door by door, in Quechua — was limited to the screening and treatment services. No one understood that their samples were being stored and used for research purposes that had nothing to do with their own health.

She asked each of the eighteen weakened patients the same question. When did it start?

Fourteen placed the beginning within six weeks of their first clinic visit.

She could name now the look Dr. Vargas had given the crowd at the opening ceremony. It was the look of a man taking inventory.

She called Adriana.

— — —

III. The Closure

Adriana came to Chinchero.

She had expected to advise by phone, the way she handled most of her cases — remotely, from Lima, in the spaces between court dates. But something in Sisa's voice when she described the foreign doctors, the untraceable registration, the samples and the weakening, had made her book a bus. She arrived on a Tuesday with a laptop and a contact in a health watchdog organization in Bogotá who had, it turned out, been looking into something similar.

They worked from Sisa's kitchen table for four days.

The first night, Sisa noticed the dog.

It was at the edge of the road outside the kitchen window — large, dark, sitting in the way dogs sit when they are waiting rather than resting. She did not have a dog. Her neighbors did not have a dog that looked like that. It was there when she noticed it at ten p.m. and still there when she checked at midnight. When she looked at one a.m., before closing the shutters, it was gone.

She did not mention it to Adriana.

What they found was not one clinic. It was a pattern — across three countries, across twelve years, always the same structure: a remote indigenous community with no health facility, a letter from an organization with a long name and a Lima or Bogotá or Quito postal box, a team of doctors whose origins no one could confirm, a program offering free care that the community received with gratitude and did not question. Always the same services. Always the blood draws and the family histories and the consent forms that said one thing in the official language and something softer and less precise in the local one.

In Ecuador, a community in the highlands near Otavalo. Four years earlier. The clinic had operated for fourteen months, then closed citing funding constraints. Several community members had reported a persistent feeling of diminishment — not illness, just less. The case had been referred to the health ministry and had gone nowhere.

In Bolivia, near Lake Titicaca. Six years ago. The pattern identical. A nurse there had filed a complaint that was still pending.

In Colombia, in an indigenous community in Nariño. Nine years ago. The clinic there had been the first, or the first they could find. The nurse who had raised concerns — Adriana found the reference in a footnote of an unpublished report from a human rights organization — had died in a road accident eight months after the clinic closed. The report did not suggest a connection. It simply noted her death in passing, as context.

Sisa read this and did not say anything for a while.

The second night, she heard footsteps on the roof.

Not loud — not like a person walking, more like the settling sound of old timber, except it moved. It began above the kitchen, traveled slowly toward the bedroom end of the house, and stopped. She lay still and listened. The altitude wind moved around the eaves. The footsteps did not repeat.

In the morning she checked the roof from the outside. The tiles were undisturbed. There were no marks in the dust on the low wall surrounding the flat section above the kitchen.

She told Adriana she had not slept well.

The parent organization, in every case, was different — a different name, a different postal address, different registrations in different countries. But the logo was the same. A stylized mountain. A caduceus. Slightly different proportions in each version, as if redrawn by hand each time — but the same image.

And the lead doctor, in each case, was described the same way. Tall. Pale. Eyes that were pleasant and difficult to read. A name that didn't quite fit.

The third night, Adriana woke Sisa at 2 a.m.

She was standing in the doorway of the bedroom, holding her phone as a light. She said she had seen someone at the kitchen window. Not clearly — a shape, a suggestion, gone by the time she reached the window. A tall shape. Pale, she said, and then corrected herself: pale-colored. I don't know. It was dark.

They sat together in the kitchen with the overhead light on until morning. Adriana worked. Sisa made coffee and looked at the window, which showed only the dark road and the mountains beyond and the faint pre-dawn brightening on the eastern peaks.

Have you been seeing things too? Adriana said, at some point.

Yes, Sisa said.

Neither of them said anything else about it.

It's the same people, Adriana said, on the fourth night, looking at the photographs the Bolivian nurse had taken at her clinic's opening ceremony. Or the same person. Or — She stopped. She was a lawyer. She did not finish sentences she couldn't support with documentation.

Or the same thing, Sisa said.

They decided to go to the clinic together the next morning. To confront Dr. Vargas directly, on the record, with what they had found. To demand documentation. To begin the formal process of making this visible.

On the fourth night, both of them slept. Sisa did not know why — perhaps because the decision had been made, or perhaps because whatever had been watching them had already made its own decision. She woke at five a.m. with the specific alertness of someone whose sleep has ended rather than been interrupted, and she lay still for a moment and felt the quality of the house around her, which was ordinary. Just her house. Just the altitude cold and the mountain sounds and the pre-dawn silence.

They went at eight a.m.

The building was empty.

Not in the way a building empties when people leave — not with the residue of departure, the forgotten items, the disorder of a hasty exit. Empty as if it had been prepared for emptiness. The equipment was gone. The freezers were gone. The filing cabinets were gone. The floors were clean. The windows had been left open, and the mountain air moved through the rooms in the particular way it moves through spaces where nothing remains to interrupt it.

On the front step, one thing: the logo, printed on a small card, weighted down by a stone. The mountain and the caduceus. No address. No name. Nothing on the back.

Sisa picked it up.

She stood in the doorway of the empty clinic and looked at the card and thought about her grandmother's instruction: You learn to see him before he sees you.

She had learned to see him. He had left anyway, because he was already finished — because whatever he had come for, he had taken, and what remained in Chinchero was not what he wanted but what he had left behind.

— — —

IV. What Remains

The village was quieter without the clinic, in the specific way of places where something has been taken. Not destroyed — reduced. The people who had weakened did not recover quickly. Some did, slowly, over months, as if whatever had been drawn from them was being replenished by the body's own stubborn processes. Some did not recover in any way Sisa could measure.

Doña Celestina still climbed to the high pastures, but less often now, and not as far.

Adriana filed what complaints she could — to bodies that had jurisdiction over organizations that no longer operated in Peru and whose principals could not be identified. She was experienced enough to know what this meant. She filed anyway, because filing was the record, and the record was the only thing that outlasted the people who created it.

Sisa kept her notebook. She kept the card with the mountain and the caduceus. She added everything she and Adriana had found — the twelve years, the three countries, the pattern, the logo, the descriptions of a tall pale man with difficult eyes — to a document she sent to the health watchdog in Bogotá and to two journalists and to a researcher at a university in Lima who studied bioethics and who wrote back immediately to say she had been tracking something similar for three years and had been unable to find anyone else who had seen what Sisa had seen.

They talked for two hours. The researcher had a name for what they were looking at. Sisa had a different name for it, older, from her grandmother's kitchen.

They were the same name.

— — —

Sisa was in her kitchen when the message came — a health sector newsletter, a brief item.

The Andean Community Health Initiative had opened a new clinic. A different village — smaller, more remote, higher altitude, more isolated. Medically underserved, the announcement said. Enthusiastic about the partnership.

It mentioned free consultations. Free vaccinations. Free prenatal care.

It included a photograph of the opening ceremony. In it, a tall man with pale eyes stood at the center of a crowd of people who were smiling. He was shaking hands with a mayor she did not recognize. Around him, the village celebrated the way people celebrate when they have been needing something for a long time and had stopped expecting it.

She looked at the photograph for a long time. The man's face was not quite Dr. Vargas's face — a different arrangement of the same features, perhaps, or just the quality of the photograph, which was slightly overexposed in the way of photographs taken in high-altitude sunlight.

She put down her phone.

She thought about her grandmother's instruction: You learn to see him before he sees you.

She picked the phone back up and called Adriana.

— — —

El Pishtaco is a figure from Andean folklore dating to the colonial period, when indigenous communities reported encounters with white outsiders who harvested human fat for use in church bells, machinery, and later pharmaceutical products. He has been continuously reinterpreted across five centuries to reflect the current form of extraction —

colonial administrators, then missionaries, then doctors, then researchers.

He is always pale. He is always from somewhere no one can quite identify. He is always welcomed at first.

The instruments change. The taking does not.

— — —

09

La Tunche

Everything the Jungle Records

Miraflores, Lima, Peru · A Monday night in August · 2026

Everything the Jungle Records

The file arrived at 11:47 p.m. on a Monday.

Valentín almost didn't open it. He had been in the edit suite since seven that morning working on a different project — a corporate documentary about water infrastructure that was aggressively boring and due Thursday — and he had been about to shut down the session and go home when the email came in. The subject line said only: Urgent audio analysis — Madre de Dios footage. The sender was a production company he had worked with twice. The body of the email was four sentences: a request, a deadline of 8 a.m. Tuesday, a note that the crew on the original shoot had not returned from the field and contact had been lost, and a request that he review the material — which had been transmitted automatically from a field backup drive before contact was lost — before anyone else heard it.

He read the email twice.

He opened the file.

It was nineteen days of raw field audio from an illegal mining documentary. Multiple tracks — ambient, boom, lavalier mics on various subjects. He skimmed the metadata. Madre de Dios, southeastern Peru. Illegal gold operations. Three-person crew plus a local fixer. Standard documentary setup.

He looked at the clock. He looked at the door. He looked at the coffee machine in the corner, which was half full and still warm from the afternoon.

The crew had not returned from the field.

He poured a cup and sat back down.

— — —

The edit suite was on the fourth floor of a building in Miraflores that had been a residential apartment block in a previous life and still had the proportions of one — low ceilings, thick walls, windows that looked out on a narrow street that was quiet after ten. The room had been acoustically treated when the building was converted: specialized panels on the walls and ceiling, a floating floor, a door with a rubber seal that made a soft sighing sound when it closed. The treatment was good. When the door was shut, the room held sound the way a sealed jar holds air — completely, with no leakage in either direction.

Valentín had worked here for four years. He knew the room's silence the way a person knows the silence of their own house — its specific quality, its texture, the particular absence of the city noise that was always present just outside the walls but never inside them. The silence of this room was his baseline. He could hear through it the way a doctor hears through a stethoscope: not the silence itself but what the silence made audible.

He put on his headphones and began.

— — —

I. The First Pass

The early material was unremarkable. Day one: river sounds, machinery, men talking in Spanish with Andean accents, the specific acoustic signature of a jungle clearing — close sounds absorbed quickly, distant sounds carrying further than they should through gaps in the canopy. Good field recording.

Whoever had done the original work knew what they were doing.

He built a rough timeline of each day's material, flagging the usable takes, noting the ambient noise floor, identifying the frequencies that would need attention in the final mix.

It was on day three that he first noticed something.

He had been boosting the low-mid frequencies to clean up a generator hum — standard practice, nothing unusual — when a signal appeared underneath the hum that he had not heard on the raw playback. A whistle. A single descending note, faint, barely above the noise floor. He cut the generator frequency and isolated the signal. It was there. Intermittent. Distant.

He made a note in his session: day 3, 14:23 — unidentified audio artifact. Possible wildlife. Flag for director.

He continued.

By day six the generator hum note in his session had twelve entries, all variations on the same description. By day eight he stopped writing possible wildlife.

He sat back and took off his headphones and looked at the acoustic panels on the wall.

The panels were dark grey, dense foam in a grid pattern. They had always reminded him of something he couldn't name — the texture of them, the way they absorbed everything that touched them. He had never thought about it long enough to arrive at the comparison.

He put his headphones back on.

— — —

II. The Second Pass

He went back to day one.

The whistle was there. He had missed it on the first pass because he had not been listening for it and because it was very faint — three, maybe four decibels above the ambient floor, which was the threshold below which most ears, even trained ones, registered a signal as part of the background rather than a discrete event. He boosted the frequency band, narrowed the window, played it again.

There. Day one, hour two, minute seven. A single descending note. Duration approximately 1.3 seconds. Then again at minute nineteen. Then again at minute forty-four.

He built a spectrogram. He looked at the waveform's shape.

He had been doing this for eleven years. He had analyzed audio from conflict zones, disaster sites, environments where unusual sounds were common and where the ability to identify and categorize them correctly had practical consequences. He had a broad reference library of sounds in his memory and a broader one in the database on his workstation. He searched the database.

No match.

He searched a secondary database, an open-source archive of jungle acoustic environments maintained by a university in Brazil. He entered the whistle's frequency profile, its duration, its decay pattern.

No match.

He sat looking at the spectrogram. The shape of the note's descent was unusual — not the smooth curve of a bird call or a human whistle, but something with a slight irregularity in the middle, a hesitation, as if whatever produced it had a specific way of breathing that expressed itself in the sound.

He had been in the suite for four hours. It was now 3:15 a.m.

He became aware, at some point during the second pass, that he had stopped blinking at his normal rate. He noticed this because his eyes were dry and he had to make a conscious effort to blink, which was the kind of noticing that happens when you have been focusing on something with an intensity that has temporarily suspended ordinary physical maintenance. He blinked. He drank the rest of his cold coffee. He looked at the acoustic panels.

The panels absorbed sound. That was their function. They were full of captured frequencies — everything that had ever been played in this room, every voice, every mix, absorbed into the foam and held there. He had never thought of this as anything other than engineering.

He looked away from the panels.

He built the timeline.

Day one through seven: the whistle present, faint, consistent. Distance — or what served as distance — stable.

Day eight through eleven: marginally louder. A fraction of a decibel per day, the kind of change that was not dramatic on any single day but was legible across the sequence.

Day twelve: a man named Aurelio went missing. Valentín found this in the production notes attached to the file, a single line: Day 12 — crew member Aurelio Quispe, local hire, missing since evening. Search conducted.

He stopped.

He read the line again. Then he scrolled through the rest of the production notes — the full document, which he had skimmed at the start and not read carefully. The document ended on day eighteen. There were no notes for day nineteen. The document itself ended mid-sentence, the final entry breaking off in the middle of a word, as if the person writing it had stopped suddenly and had not come back.

He thought about the email. The crew had not returned from the field. Three people and a fixer. The audio had been transmitted automatically from a backup drive. No one had sent it. It had sent itself, the way backup systems do when they detect a loss of connection to the source device — a final transmission, the last thing the drive did before the connection went dead.

He was listening to the recordings of people who were gone.

He put on his headphones and played day twelve.

The whistle hit him before he was ready for it.

Not the faint signal he had been isolating and boosting — this was present in the raw audio, no enhancement needed, no frequency manipulation. It came through the headphones at a level that made him flinch and reach for the output fader before he caught himself. Not loud enough to damage — but loud enough to be wrong, loud enough to be the kind of sound that arrived in the ear differently from other sounds, that seemed to bypass the normal pathway from eardrum to brain and go somewhere more direct. He played it again with the gain reduced.

Still wrong. Still that quality of directness.

Underneath the sound of men calling a name into the dark, the whistle descended. Once. Twice. Three times in four minutes. Each time the same note, the same descent, the same irregularity in the middle — but fuller now, present in a way the earlier recordings were not. As if whatever had been producing it at a distance had moved. Or decided to stop pretending distance was relevant.

Day thirteen: louder. He pulled the headphones off after the first occurrence, which came at minute four of the morning session, sudden and close and wrong in the way that sounds are wrong when they exist in a register your body recognizes before your mind does. He sat with the headphones around his neck and his pulse elevated and his hands flat on the console until his breathing settled. Then he put them back on.

Day fourteen: he turned the output gain to its lowest usable setting before pressing play. It was not low enough. The whistle came at minute nine and minute twenty-two and minute forty-one, each time the same note but each time with something added — a texture beneath the descent, a resonance that his equipment could not fully reproduce, that he could hear the edges of but not the center of, that his ear kept reaching for and not finding. He stopped the playback after the third occurrence and sat with his eyes closed.

Day fifteen: the whistle began at minute one. He had barely pressed play. He pulled the headphones off and held them in his lap and listened to the recording through the suite's monitors at low volume instead, which was better — the room's acoustic treatment scattered the sound, softened its edges, made it something he could observe rather than something that was happening directly inside his head.

Through the monitors, at low volume, across the room: still wrong. Still that quality. But manageable.

Day sixteen, seventeen, eighteen through the monitors, volume reduced.

Day eighteen: the recording stopped mid-session at 17:43. In the fourteen seconds before the cut, the whistle was at its highest recorded level — through the monitors, at the lowest volume setting he could use while still technically hearing anything, it filled the room with a frequency he felt in his back teeth and behind his eyes before the file terminated and the silence of the suite rushed back in.

He sat in the silence for a full minute before touching anything.

Day nineteen: no audio file.

Valentín sat with this.

— — —

III. What the Room Held

It was 4:40 a.m. when he first heard it in the room.

He had his headphones off — resting his ears, staring at the spectrogram. The suite was in its full acoustic isolation: rubber-sealed door, floating floor, panels absorbing everything. He had been in this silence ten thousand times. He knew its exact texture.

Which was how he knew, immediately and without doubt, that what he heard was inside the room with him.

A single descending note. Barely above the threshold of perception. The same irregularity in the middle, the same hesitation. Not from the headphones — the headphones were on the console. Not from the monitors — the monitors were off. From the room. From somewhere the acoustic treatment made impossible to locate, the sound arriving at him from multiple angles at once.

He sat very still.

He told himself: bleed-through. An anomaly in the building. He had reported it to the building manager twice. He waited for the silence to reassert itself.

At 4:52, it came again.

Same note. Same descent. Louder — not by much, but by exactly the fraction he had documented each day in the Madre de Dios footage. He recognized the increment. He had spent four hours learning to recognize it.

He took the headphones carefully off the console and placed them on his head. He turned the gain to zero. He looked at the input meters.

They were moving.

The meters were picking up the whistle inside the room. The room's own microphone — used for reference recordings, rarely active, always present — was capturing it. It was real. It was in the air. The meters confirmed it in the flat green language of digital certainty, a signal registering at the same frequency he had been documenting across nineteen days, climbing the meter in small precise increments that matched his timeline exactly.

He pressed record.

He did not know why he pressed record. Some reflex, some professional instinct older than his fear.

At 5:04 it came again.

Louder. Not marginally — significantly. The meters jumped. He put his hands over the headphones — they were still at zero gain, he heard nothing through them, but he put his hands over them anyway, a reflex that had nothing to do with reasoning. The note descended and held at the bottom for a fraction longer than it had before, that bottom frequency sitting in the air of the sealed room and in his chest simultaneously, a resonance he felt behind his ribs before it faded.

He stood up so fast his chair rolled back and hit the wall.

He looked at the door. Sealed. Green indicator light. Performing within specification.

He looked at the acoustic panels. Grey foam, dense, four years of captured frequencies. He had never once thought of the panels as containing anything. Sound in, silence out. Physics. Engineering.

He looked at the input meters, which had returned to their resting state. The signal was gone.

He sat back down. He pulled up the recording he had just made. There it was on the waveform — three occurrences, clean, documented, timestamped. He looked at the waveform of the third occurrence, the one at 5:04.

He zoomed in.

The shape of the descent was identical to the day eighteen recording. Not similar. Identical. The same irregularity in the same position, the same duration to the millisecond, the same resonant texture at the bottom of the note's range. He put them side by side on the screen — day eighteen from Madre de Dios, his own recording from three minutes ago — and he looked at them until his eyes hurt.

At 5:11 it came again.

And this time it was not gradual. This time it arrived at a level that sent him backward in his chair with his hands over his ears, the sound filling the sealed room from every direction at once, not a whistle anymore in any ordinary sense but something that used the shape of a whistle the way weather uses the shape of a door — something passing through a form too small for it, the pressure of it distorting the form, the descent of the note dropping through frequencies his equipment could capture and then through frequencies below that, frequencies he felt in his jaw and his sinuses and the base of his skull before the sound cut off.

Complete silence.

He sat in his chair with his hands still over his ears and his heart doing something he could feel in his temples.

He lowered his hands.

He looked at the screen. The waveform of the 5:11 occurrence was clipping — the meter had maxed out and held there for the duration of the note. In twenty-three years of working with audio, he had never seen a sound clip a meter in an acoustically treated room with no source.

He stood up again, steadier this time.

He opened the project file manager. He selected all nineteen audio files. He selected his own recording from the last thirty minutes.

He pressed delete.

The system asked him to confirm. He confirmed.

He closed the session without saving. He opened his email client. He found the message from the production company and replied:

I'm sorry — I don't appear to have received any files from you, and I won't be able to take on this project. I hope you find someone who can help.

He sent it. He put on his coat. He picked up his bag. He turned off the monitors. He turned off the workstation.

He opened the door, which made its soft sighing sound, and stepped into the hallway, and pulled the door firmly shut behind him.

He stood in the hallway.

He could hear nothing from inside the room.

He walked to the elevator. He pressed the button. He waited with his hands in his pockets and the email sitting in his outbox and the particular quality of a person who has made a decision and is moving through the aftermath of it before they have had time to examine what they have decided.

The elevator arrived. He got in. The doors closed.

He got out on the ground floor and walked through the lobby and pushed through the glass door and stepped into the street.

The night air was cold and damp. The Pacific a few blocks away. A delivery truck at the far end of the road. A dog on a doorstep. The first grey light above the buildings to the east.

He stood on the pavement and breathed.

He did not hear anything except the truck, receding, and the city beginning its morning.

He told himself this was because the room was sealed.

He told himself this was because he had deleted the files.

He walked to the corner and kept walking — toward the bus stop, toward home, toward the ordinary requirements of a Tuesday that had not yet begun and would not ask him about anything he did not want to answer.

— — —

The Madre de Dios region of southeastern Peru contains one of the largest illegal gold mining operations in the world. An estimated 30,000 to 40,000 miners work its river systems using mercury extraction methods that have contaminated waterways, destroyed rainforest, and displaced indigenous communities across hundreds of thousands of hectares. Hundreds of workers disappear each year. Most are recorded as accidents.

La Tunche is a spirit of the Amazon jungle. It announces itself with a whistle — a single descending note, heard at dusk or in the dark, from inside the trees. Volume and distance do not correspond. This detail is consistent across every recorded version of the story.

In some versions, hearing it is the last warning before it arrives.

In others, hearing it means it has already decided.

The distinction, those who have studied the legend note, may be academic.

— — —

10

El Caleuche

The Light on the Water

Golfo de Ancud, Chiloé, Chile · July · 2026

The Light on the Water

She had not wanted the midnight shift.

Nobody wanted the midnight shift at the Ancud coast guard station, which was why it belonged to the newest officer, which was why it belonged to Lieutenant Sofía Aravena — twenty-six years old, eight weeks out of the academy, assigned to Chiloé because she had finished third in her class and third meant you chose your specialty but not your location.

The shift ran midnight to eight. The station was small: a console, a radar screen, a radio, a window facing the bay. She was alone, six nights a week, in the specific silence of a place that has been awake when everything around it is asleep. She had been doing it for six weeks when she saw the ship for the first time.

— — —

I. The First Night

A radar contact at 2:14 a.m. Northeast bearing, three kilometers offshore, sixty seconds, then gone.

She checked the equipment. All within parameters. She logged it as an anomaly and went back to the water infrastructure report she had been filing and did not think about it again.

Not during the shift, anyway.

— — —

II. The Second Night

The same contact appeared the following Tuesday. Same bearing, same distance. This time she was watching.

The glow came first — diffuse, low on the water, warm in a way that July water in the Golfo de Ancud had no business being. She was standing at the window, hands on the sill, when it reached her.

Later she would not be able to say how it happened. One moment she was at the window looking at the water. The next she was somewhere else entirely — on a deck, warm air around her, the smell of wood and salt and something like food being prepared. People around her, easy with each other, laughing at something she had not heard. A man near her turned and looked at her with recognition — there you are — the look of someone who had been waiting for her specifically, who was glad she had arrived.

She had not felt that since the academy. She had not felt that in Ancud at all.

She was reaching toward the man when something snagged at the edge of her vision. Below, through a gap in the deck planking — a face looking up. Young. A woman her own age, eyes wide, mouth slightly open, the expression of someone who wanted very badly to speak and had understood that speaking would not help.

Then she was at the window again. The glow was gone. The water was empty. The radar contact had dropped.

She was gripping the windowsill with both hands.

She looked at the clock. Fourteen minutes had passed.

She sat down. She did not log what she had seen. She told herself: the midnight shift, six weeks in, she had been half-asleep. The mind makes things.

— — —

III. The Third Night

She went to the window when the contact appeared, at 0:43 a.m. and closer — two and a half kilometers this time. She went because she had been thinking about the warmth all week. The man who had looked at her with recognition. She had not admitted this to herself while thinking it.

The transition was faster this time.

The deck — the people — the warmth. But now she could see it more clearly. A gathering, a celebration of some kind. The kind of ease that comes from belonging somewhere completely, from having arrived at a place and been kept. She moved through the people and they made room for her with the natural accommodation of a group that has space for one more.

This was what it looked like, she thought, to have chosen correctly.

Then the music changed pitch for just a second — a half-tone shift, something going wrong inside it — and she looked toward the sound and saw, through an open hatch in the deck, steep stairs going down into the hold. She could see only the top steps but she could see enough: the quality of the light below was different, colder, functional in the way of a space that was not meant to be lived in but was. And a hand on the stair rail — young, gripping the railing from below, trying to stay visible.

Someone was trying to come up.

The hatch closed.

She was at the window. Rain on the glass. The water empty. Her breath fogging the pane.

She filed a routine patrol report and went home at eight a.m. and slept badly and did not eat until afternoon and thought about the hand on the stair rail and told herself it was a dream and nearly believed it.

— — —

IV. The Fourth Night

Two kilometers. The music before the glow this time — she heard it inside the station, sourceless, while the contact was still forming on the radar. She was at the window before she had decided to be there.

The deck opened around her like a room she had always known the layout of.

There were faces she recognized this time. She had grown up in Valparaíso, had left it for the academy, had tried not to miss it, had missed it constantly. The ship showed her: a kitchen she knew, her mother at a counter, her younger sister at the table with her books spread out the way she always spread them, covering everything. Saturday morning. Coffee. The specific light that came through the east-facing window in the morning.

She stood in it and felt the specific grief of a person who is homesick and has been pretending they are not.

Then her sister looked up from her books.

Her sister's face was wrong. Not frightened — empty. The way a face is empty when it has been looking at the same four walls for a very long time. And the kitchen — she looked at it again — was not quite her kitchen. The walls were close. There were no windows after all. There had never been windows. It was a room that had been made to look like a kitchen, that had been assembled from her memories with just enough accuracy to pass.

She tried to say her sister's name.

The scene dissolved. She was at the window. The rain. The water.

She stood there for a long time with her hand flat against the glass, feeling the cold of it, the solid fact of it, the realness of it.

She went to the console. She wrote: 0147 hrs — contact northeast 2.0 km, duration 40 min. She stopped. Deleted. Wrote: routine patrol, all clear.

She put on her coat.

She told herself she was going to document the vessel from the patrol boat. She was a coast guard officer. This was her duty.

She almost believed it.

— — —

V. The Last Night

She took the patrol boat out alone, without logging the departure.

The water was black and very cold, the swells long and authoritative. She cut the engine at five hundred meters and let the boat drift. The glow was close now — closer than it had ever been from the station window, close enough that the warmth of it was real, physical, reaching her across the water.

The music. And then — not gradually, not with the soft approach of the previous nights — the deck simply appeared around her, full and immediate, and she was on it, and the ship was real under her feet, the planking solid and worn and salt-stiffened, and the people were real.

For one moment it was everything it had shown her. Warmth, belonging, the ease of people who were somewhere they had chosen.

Then she took a step and something shifted.

The glow changed — from warm to cold and functional. The sound of the music was replaced by the sound of the ship as it actually was: the creak of stressed wood, the bilge moving, voices below the deck that were not the voices of celebration. She looked at the people around her and they were not what they had been. They were young — many of them very young, some no older than sixteen — sitting against the rails in the cramped specific posture of people who have been in the same position for too long and know they will be in it longer. Some were asleep the way people sleep when sleep is the only available escape. Some watched her with expressions that held no welcome. That held only exhaustion, and the residue of hope, and the specific wariness of people who have learned not to trust what the ship shows you.

A girl sitting against the rail said quietly, in the accent of Chiloé: Run.

A hand closed around Sofía's arm from behind.

She spun. A man — the flat efficiency of someone for whom this was a task, a logistics problem, nothing more. He looked at her uniform without expression. His grip did not tighten or loosen. It simply held.

She reached for her radio.

It was in the cradle of the patrol boat, which she could see between the rail and the water — drifting, the current pulling it south, already beyond reach, small and dark and getting smaller with the specific indifference of a thing that has been let go of.

She looked at the water. At the distance. At the girl against the rail who had stopped looking at her, who had turned her face toward the hull.

The man said, in Spanish with no accent she could place: "Welcome aboard."

He was not welcoming her.

The Caleuche continued northeast, as it always had, through the Golfo de Ancud and into the open Pacific and beyond, into the jurisdictions and the dark, carrying what it carried.

— — —

Lieutenant Sofía Aravena was reported missing when she did not answer the station radio at the end of her shift. The patrol boat was found drifting two kilometers offshore, engine off, radio in its cradle. The log showed a final entry: 0147 hrs — routine patrol, all clear. Timestamped eleven days earlier.

The search found nothing. The case was filed as accident, officer overboard, body not recovered.

The midnight shift was given to the civilian contractor who was fifty-three and had worked this posting for eleven years and read novels at the console until dawn and had never once, in eleven years, looked at the window.

— — —

The Chiloé archipelago has been a transit point for human trafficking networks for over two decades. Young people from coastal fishing communities are disproportionately targeted. Coast guard resources in the region are significantly understaffed relative to the maritime area they cover.

El Caleuche is a ghost ship from Chiloé folklore — a vessel that appears at night in the Golfo de Ancud, glowing, with music and lights. Those who board are never seen again. It has been reported continuously for three hundred years.

The oldest versions say it does not take everyone. It approaches, night after night, until it finds the one it has decided on. It shows that person what they most want to see.

Then it shows them what it is.

— — —

A Note on the Legends / Nota sobre las Leyendas

Each story in this collection is built around a legend from Latin American folklore. These notes are intended to be read after the stories, not before.

La Llorona — *Mexico and throughout Latin America*

The Weeping Woman is one of the oldest and most widespread legends in the Americas, predating the Spanish conquest in some versions. Along the US-Mexico border, she has become not only a ghost but a witness — and, some say, a warning.

El Cadejo — *Guatemala, El Salvador, Honduras, Mexico*

A supernatural dog — or two dogs, one white, one black — that follows travelers at night. The white Cadejo protects; the black Cadejo destroys. The legend is inseparable from the dangerous roads of Central America.

La Viuda — *Panama*

The Widow appears to corrupt men at night. In Panamanian folklore she is connected to financial and moral corruption — a figure who makes what is hidden visible, who extracts from the corrupt a reckoning they cannot escape.

La Sayona — *Venezuela, Colombia*

A vengeful woman who appears to those who harm women and children. The legend speaks directly to the rates of femicide and gender violence that have characterized Venezuela for decades.

El Silbón — *Venezuela, Colombia*

A whistling figure who wanders the Llanos carrying a sack of bones, cursed forever as punishment for patricide. The whistle sounds close when it is far, and far when it is close. When you can no longer hear it, it is beside you.

La Madremonte — *Colombia*

The Mother of the Mountain is a guardian of the Colombian rainforest — a figure who drives away or destroys those who damage the land. She appears most often in stories from regions under threat from logging, mining, and agricultural expansion.

El Familiar — *Argentina, Bolivia*

A demon associated with large sugar estates. The owner makes a pact: prosperity in exchange for a periodic human sacrifice, typically a new worker unknown to the community. Labor historians note the legend emerged simultaneously with the industrial sugar economy and the large-scale importation of migrant labor.

El Pishtaco — *Peru, Bolivia*

One of the oldest Andean legends, dating to the colonial period. A white outsider who harvests from indigenous bodies — originally fat for church bells and machinery, later reinterpreted in each century to reflect the current form of extraction. The instruments change. The taking does not.

La Tunche — *Peru, Bolivia*

A spirit of the Amazon jungle that announces itself with a whistle — a single descending note. Volume and distance do not correspond. This detail is consistent across every recorded version of the story.

El Caleuche — *Chile*

A ghost ship from the island of Chiloé — a vessel that appears at night in the Golfo de Ancud, glowing, with music and lights. Those who board are never seen again. It has been reported continuously for three hundred years. It shows that person what they most want to see. Then it shows them what it is.

Acknowledgments / Agradecimientos

These stories could not have been written without the scholars, journalists, human rights workers, and community members who have documented the conditions they describe — often at considerable personal risk. The footnotes at the end of each story point toward that documentation.

I am also indebted to the communities that have carried these legends across generations, that have kept them alive and kept them honest, that have continued to find in old stories the language for new harms.

Any errors of fact, interpretation, or representation are mine.

About the Author / Sobre el Autor

Arturo Cova was born in Peru, grew up between two worlds, and eventually chose a third — the United States, where he lived long enough to understand what it means to leave a place and carry it with you anyway.

He served as a Peace Corps volunteer in Nicaragua. He has worked in communities across Latin America. He took the name of a man who walked into the jungle and did not come back.

He began this collection in 2012. He is somewhere in Latin America.

— — —

Ecos del Miedo / Echoes of Fear

www.ingramcontent.com/pod-product-compliance
Lightning Source LLC
LaVergne TN
LVHW010948110826
845149LV00015B/3266

9798995512714